JUST A BOY

ALSO BY
MAEVE HENRY

MAEVE HENRY

JUST A BOY

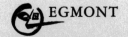

EGMONT

For Daniel

First published in Great Britain 2001 by Egmont Books Ltd
239 Kensington High Street, London W8 6SA

Text copyright © 2001 Maeve Henry
Cover illustration copyright © 2001 Christopher Gibbs

The moral rights of the author and cover illustrator have been asserted

ISBN 0 7497 4684 X

10 9 8 7 6 5 4 3 2

A CIP catalogue record for this title is available from the British Library

Typeset by Avon DataSet Ltd, Bidford on Avon, Warwickshire
Printed in Great Britain by
Cox & Wyman Ltd, Reading, Berkshire

Contents

Foreword

This story is set in and around the village of Church Gresley in Derbyshire in the 1870s.

It was a place of smoky industry, of coal mines and potteries, surrounded by wooded hills and open farmland. Life was a struggle then for ordinary families. Men and women worked for long hours for very little, and children left school early to earn their keep. Disease or industrial accident wiped out many breadwinners, and left families facing complete destitution.

This is the story of one family at that time, and of one boy in particular: Enoch Kirk, my great-grandfather – just a boy.

PART ONE

'The devil's in that child!'

1

A hungry stomach

Enoch Kirk, aged four, was standing in the middle of
the red-tiled kitchen floor, staring at the unlit kitchen
range. It was early afternoon on a raw November day
and without a lamp or a candle the small room was in
gloomy twilight. Enoch had rolled down the sleeves of
his shirt so that the cuffs hung several inches beyond
his fingertips and he had tugged at the ragged jumper
till it reached his knees, but he was still cold. He was
hungry, too, with a gnawing pain that left him restless
and angry. There had been only thin porridge last
night, and nothing this morning, nothing for the rest
of the day till his mother came home. The damp chill
off the tiles struck his bare feet and calves cruelly. He
ought to have been upstairs in the back bedroom with

Daniel, curled under the blankets against his brother's warm side, but Daniel had fallen into one of his queer moods when he read aloud from the Bible and cried about his legs. Enoch had scrambled under the bed and refused to come out. Daniel had raged and shouted until at last he had fallen asleep and Enoch had crept downstairs.

There was nothing to eat in any of the cupboards. That was the first thing he had tried. The flour crock was empty. There was no dripping in the pan. Downstairs there was nothing to play with except the furniture, four scuffed chairs round the battered table. It looked like furniture saved from a shipwreck, Enoch thought. There was a story about a wreck in one of Daniel's old school readers, but Enoch could only pick out a word or two. When Daniel woke up, he might be able to get him to read the story. He turned and padded out into the scullery. Here the cold was worse, biting at his bare feet so painfully that he began to whimper. He went back into the kitchen and sat down on the worn rag rug, fingering its hard grey and black and brown coils. Daniel had told him of seeing it made. In those days, when clothes got too old to wear, new ones were bought. There had been a clock on the mantelpiece, and two china shepherdesses, Daniel said. He liked to talk about those days. There had been food in the house, and a good fire, and a tablecloth. There had been more family at home too, his sister Polly, another sister and another brother. Enoch couldn't understand where everything had gone, the good times and the Sunday dinners, and the china shepherdesses. He wasn't sure if he believed Daniel. There was only a box of matches on the mantelpiece now.

Seeing it gave him an idea. He fetched a chair, snatched the matches and jumped down again. He pulled out a match and dragged it along the box like his mother did. The flame spurted blue, then turned a steady yellow. Just before it reached his fingers the flame flickered and died. Enoch dropped it into the grate, and put the box carefully on the chair. Coal first, he had remembered.

He knew he wasn't to touch the coal in the coal scuttle. That made a mess, and got his hands scrubbed furiously and his ears boxed. But there was other coal outside, through the back door in the lean-to shed. But out in the yard the mud demanded his immediate attention. It allowed his feet to slide bumpily over the cobbles; his hands too. Under his fingers the cobbles were cold and sleek, like the body of a dog in the rain. He looked up and there was a real dog, a lurcher, sniffing at the doors of the privies opposite. As the lurcher sidled along the doors, a man came out of one of them. He was a miner, his face tattooed with coal grains looking blue under the skin. He kicked the lurcher, yelping, out of his path, and stamped away.

Short time, Enoch remembered. That was what Daniel said it was called. The miners stood on the corner of the street half the day, or shouted at their wives at home so you could hear it through the walls on either side. He held his breath till the man had gone, then squatted down in the yard and called to the injured dog. The animal pricked up its ears and got to its feet. Enoch called again. The lurcher hesitated, then trotted towards him. Enoch allowed it to sniff round him, then very gently put his hand up to its neck and patted the rough hair. The lurcher was a dull brown colour, wet and muddy. Its muzzle was greying and the whites of its eyes had a yellow tinge.

'Poor old dog,' said Enoch, running his hand along the lurcher's shivering back. 'Poor old thing, aren't you?'

The animal suddenly jerked up its head. There was a hoarse bark from the tunnel that, halfway down the yard, led out into the street. Another dog, a bow-legged dirty white mongrel, came into sight. The hair rose on the back of the lurcher. His legs stiffened. Enoch removed his hand from the animal's back and stood away. A growl vibrated in the mongrel's throat.

Suddenly the two dogs leapt at each other. Enoch watched in admiration and terror as they snapped and plunged and yelped around the yard. Then the stranger leapt away, howling down the tunnel. The lurcher stood still, panting, in the middle of the yard. Then with a yelp he gave chase and Enoch was left by himself.

For a few moments he was aware of emptiness, the cheep of sparrows and the blank grey sky. Then the gnawing pain in his stomach began again. Suddenly he remembered. If he went down the tunnel to the corner of the street, his sister Polly might be there. He wiped his nose on his dangling sleeve and set off.

He tried to remember the last time he had seen Polly. It had not been so cold, that was certain, and it had been later in the day, almost dusk, the time when Mam came home from work. Polly had been waiting on the corner, and when she saw him, she held out her arms and smiled. It was that he remembered, more than the bread she brought out of her apron pocket, the wrapped up scraps of bacon or cheese. Polly loved him. She stood on that corner, not every day, sometimes not for weeks, but she came. He asked why she never came to the house.

'Mam won't let me,' she said cheerfully. 'She can't stop me seeing you here, though.'

He didn't know where Polly went when she wasn't at the corner. It didn't seem important when she was there, giving him a cuddle, and when she was gone he couldn't ask her. He never said anything at home about meeting her. He didn't even say her name in front of Mam, not unless he wanted his head clipped.

He walked quickly down the tunnel, and came out on the big street at the front. Here there were children his age sitting on doorsteps, or playing in the street with bits of stick and rag. The big ones were at school, or working. One boy was eating a thick slice of bread, swinging his legs on the step with the pleasure of it. Enoch's mouth filled with water.

He was slowing down now. In a moment he would reach the corner. He half shut his eyes, squinting ahead. It was dark at the end of the street, in the shadow of the big chimneys of the terracotta factory. There might be a person there, someone as thin as Polly, with her shawl covering her fair hair. But when he got there, it was empty. Nowhere else ever felt so empty. He waited for a long time, but Polly didn't come. Then he turned and walked back slowly past the playing children.

The hunger was so bad now he was starting to feel sick and faint. He wished he had never come out. He wished he was home again. He walked slower and slower, and came to a stop. Sullenly he stared around him, then his face brightened. He remembered this house. His mother had called in here once on a Sunday, on the way to church. The woman on the doorstep had asked her to step inside, quite friendly. Then Enoch's mother began to talk to her in that stiff hard voice, taking a little tract out of her bag, pushing it into the woman's hand. The woman had stopped being friendly then. While they were shouting, Enoch slid away to the table where, among used plates and cups, stood half a loaf and a pot of meat paste. His mother's hand shot out and pulled him back. Not long after that, they left.

Enoch thought of that meat paste, the rich smell and texture of it. He was so hungry that somehow he knew it would still be there, along with the loaf and the pretty blue and white plates. He went over to the window of the house and peered in, but it was wet with condensation and he couldn't see anything. Hunger made him foolish, careless of trouble. He went to the door and tried the handle. It wasn't locked. He eased it open an inch, then pushed it wider. There was no sound or movement from inside. He slid sideways into the back kitchen that smelled of soap and damp. He stood there, his heart pounding. The tin bath on a nail, the sink and the whitewashed walls were identical to those at home. But from behind the door he could feel warmth. There were smells of last night's cooking. If he was to be a thief, at least he had chosen the right place to steal from. He took a deep breath and pushed open the kitchen door. His eyes raked the kitchen table and he gave a howl of disappointment. There was nothing on the table but a brown bottle, a rag and a cup without a handle. He ran forward with his fists clenched. He could not manage without something in his stomach. It clamoured at him, clamoured – he grabbed the bottle and poured it into the cup. The liquid was treacly with an oily sheen, but it smelt familiar, a pleasant furniture smell like church. He gulped it down in two mouthfuls and smiled as an unusual warmth began to spread through him. Then he trembled violently. His face went cold and then hot, a spasm shook him and he began to retch. Someone came clattering down the stairs and he was lifted off his feet and carried, his face pressed against a bulging sack apron, into the scullery. He was held over the sink until the vomiting was over. Then the woman wiped his face, made him drink a little water, and carried him, still trembling, back to Daniel.

'How'm I going to polish my dresser now, eh,

Enoch? Shall I take you home again and use you as a polishing rag?'

Her hand came down and tumbled his hair, and Enoch twisted his face up to her warm palm.

But as soon as she was gone, Daniel fetched him a hard slap across the head.

'That's for sneaking into other people's houses.'

Enoch accepted it without protest.

'And that –' said Daniel, following it with another, 'is for going into Mrs Burden's.'

'Why shouldn't I, then?' Enoch wailed.

'Because she's no better than she ought to be, and Mam says we don't mix with her sort.'

'What sort?'

Daniel grinned.

'I'll tell you when you're older,' he promised. He pushed himself higher up against the pillow and put his arm round Enoch.

'You should stay in the house,' he said, gently this time. 'I know it's boring. But look, it's getting dark already and that means in a couple of hours Mam'll be home, and there'll be supper.'

'Porridge again,' said Enoch, making a face.

'It'll stop your stomach aching, though. And it'll be warm downstairs, and you can lie on the rug like a little cat.'

Enoch laughed at that. He reached up to his brother's face and gently touched his shadowy moustache.

'Are you a man or a boy, Dan?'

'A man,' said Daniel. 'More or less.'

Enoch studied him. Daniel was a boy, but there wasn't anything boyish about him. He was too white and thin. His face had a quiet look about it because he had nothing to do all day except think. Enoch touched Daniel's head. His dark hair was cut short, but the curl still came out at the front. At the back it was all matted where he lay on it, day after day.

'Come on,' Daniel grumbled. 'I'm not a dolly for you to play with.'

Enoch lay back against his arm, content that Daniel was feeling better. The bit of excitement with Mrs Burden had done him good.

'Shall I get out my trumpet and play something for you?' Daniel offered.

He reached down to where he kept it, in a small tin trunk without a lid.

'No. Tell me a story,' demanded Enoch. 'About when you worked down the pit with Dad.'

Daniel blew out his cheeks, the way he always did. He glanced at Enoch, and then began.

'Well, a long time ago, before you were born, and I was a strong lad of twelve, Dad and me worked together. I liked being with him, but I didn't like going in the mine. It was that long climb down into the dark. It's not dark like night-time, or under the bedclothes. It's a dark that seems to come inside you. Dad knew how I felt about it, and he used to whistle as we walked down to the seam. He'd whistle and count the lamps for me, till I knew we were nearly there. And once we started I was all right. It's a long day, though. In winter we started before it was light and finished long after it was dark again. I used to think that was why Sunday was called Sunday, till Dad told me different. It's a shame you never knew him, Enoch.'

Enoch murmured something sleepily, and curled closer to Daniel's side. As Daniel talked gently on, Enoch fell asleep.

'Daniel!'

It was Mam's voice outside on the stairs.

'Daniel, is Enoch up there? I've got to get him fed and washed. Have you forgotten? It's the Bible meeting tonight.'

Enoch opened his eyes to find the room in darkness. The glow of a candle suddenly lit up Daniel's face next to him.

'Go on,' said Daniel. 'You'd best be quick. You're hungry, remember? And if she has to come up and fetch you down –'

Enoch jumped quickly out of the warm bed, and ran to the door.

'I'm coming, Mam!'

2

Soap and the Bible

He stood in the tin bath in the back kitchen, naked and shivering in the candlelight, while his mother went to the bottom of the steps to call to Daniel. 'Dan, I'll send him up with a clean nightshirt in a minute.'

His legs were wet and slippery with soap. It was almost impossible to stand still, but if he shifted his feet she had told him he would slip and hurt himself. 'Stop fidgeting, you little heathen.'

One hard hand grasped him by the left shoulder, while the other scrubbed at his back and neck with the soapy rag. Then she stooped over him, the edge of her corset catching him under his ear while she rubbed his face and briskly assaulted his rib cage. He was too breathless to howl when she sluiced him down with a bucket of warm water, pummelled him with a towel and fastened him, glowing, into his Sunday shirt and trousers. She led him to stand by the fire while she combed his wet hair. Then he did start to cry as she tugged savagely at the knots.

'Now stand still and just stop snivelling while I look at you.'

Frowning, she stared down at him, a thin freckled woman with a face worn into lines, wearing her grey Sunday dress under a wet sacking apron.

'Oh, you'll do,' she said reluctantly. Something in him always fretted her, Enoch knew.

'Don't just stand there gaping, now. Take your brother up his nightshirt.'

He set off upstairs at a run, smarting inside and needing the comfort of Dan. His mother watched him go with a lingering look of dissatisfaction. Then she remembered to take off her apron, and hung it behind the back kitchen door. She walked nervously about the room, pushing the hairpins firmly up into her knot of hair. In five minutes they would be slipping again, she knew. But at least the room looked decent with a good fire, and the borrowed tea set gleaming hospitably on the table. Upstairs she could hear Daniel play something fast and noisy on the trumpet, and Enoch give a high-pitched squeal of laughter in response. She winced, wondering whether Dan would get the boy too excited to behave himself. But she had no intention of sending him to bed before the meeting. God knew Enoch needed to pray more than most.

There was a loud rapping at the front door. Ellen Kirk jumped. Her hands went to her hair again, then she rushed to open it. The door, so rarely used, was stiff, and she had half a minute of panicky struggle before she succeeded in wrenching it open. Enoch, coming downstairs, saw Mr Dawson, the new vicar, step inside and make for the fire, rubbing his hands briskly.

'Splendid! Splendid!' the vicar murmured as he gazed round the room.

Mr Dawson made exactly the same sort of vicar noises as fat old Mr Rolandson, Enoch observed, for all he looked so different. Mr Dawson was undersized and his hair was thin and well-greased. His arms and legs were like pipe-cleaners. The only impressive thing about him was his nose, which stuck out large, crooked and shiny in his flat pale face. And Enoch soon saw that his mother was going to make the same fuss over Mr Dawson as she had over Mr Rolandson.

'We're so grateful to you for coming out on such a raw evening,' she began.

Mr Dawson nodded, and began to struggle out of his heavy black overcoat.

'It's nice and warm in here, though, Mrs Kirk. Very warm.'

The overcoat didn't want to come off. Enoch tried not to laugh as Mr Dawson started flailing his arms, like a beetle that had fallen on its back.

'I'm stuck,' he said in surprise. 'Something's caught. The sleeves are so very narrow.'

Enoch's mother tried pulling the coat at the shoulders.

'No, it's stuck here,' said Mr Dawson, irritably, holding his arms up in the air. So Ellen Kirk yanked hard at his cuffs in turn, and at last the coat came off. Mr Dawson, rather red in the face, smoothed down his hair and his waistcoat.

'It looked like you were taking off a baby's jumper, Mam!' said Enoch in delight.

Mr Dawson glared at him.

'Oughtn't that child to be in bed?' he asked frostily.

But Ellen Kirk shook her head.

'Enoch needs the Word of God,' she said loudly. 'He needs to pray, and be prayed for, Mr Dawson.'

'But surely,' Mr Dawson spluttered, 'he's too young to follow the discussion. He'll simply become a nuisance.'

'Let him try,' said Ellen Kirk, looking meaningfully at Enoch. 'Just let him try.'

Mr Dawson was prevented from further argument by another knock, this time at the back door. The neighbours were arriving.

First to come in was Mr Spraggs, an elderly bachelor with a puffy face the colour of wet clay. Enoch's eyes widened as he caught the rattling wheeze of Mr Spragg's chest. Dan said it was because of the flint dust that got into his lungs at the pottery where he worked. But Enoch could hear little voices groaning and screaming as the potter drew breath and was half-afraid that Mr Spraggs was possessed by devils. Mr Dawson and Enoch's mother both moved to help him and the business of settling his heavy frame in a chair, and fetching him a reviving drink of water occupied them all for a little while.

'Raw night,' Mr Spraggs observed, when he had enough breath to speak.

'Very good of you to make the effort,' returned Mr Dawson warmly.

'Please, Mr Dawson, do sit down,' said Ellen Kirk. 'Here, by the fire, out of the draughts.'

She was standing herself, twisting her hands into anxious knots.

Mr Dawson backed obediently on to one of the

kitchen chairs. He took out his handkerchief and mopped his face. He put a finger in his shiny white collar and pulled at it. Enoch watched him, fascinated by his red sweaty face and his look of discomfort.

Silence fell. The grown-ups stared at their laps or the wall. Enoch glanced from face to face, twisting in his chair until his mother frowned at him to stop. At last, Mr Dawson cleared his throat.

'Shall we make the presumption that no one else is going to –'

But the back door rattled and banged shut and old Mrs Liverstitch burst in on them.

Enoch gave a cry of pleasure at the sight of her.

'Mam never said you were coming!'

Her answering smile was worth more than Mam's angry shushing.

'So sorry, Vicar, so sorry, Mrs Kirk, I know how you hate being kept waiting,' she said cheerfully.

Enoch watched with familiar delight as she unwound the yards of dingy woollen comforter from around her head and shoulders.

'Just a minute while I rearrange myself,' she told Enoch, tugging at her hat and her black crocheted shawl. Then she took the seat next to him, gave him a wink, and patted her broad lap. In an instant, Enoch had scrambled on to it, and wriggled round till he was comfortable. She felt in her pocket and handed him a peppermint, ignoring his mother's glare of disapproval.

'I thought you'd be in bed,' she said to Enoch, but he knew better than to reply because Mr Dawson was beginning the prayer.

Enoch kept his eyes screwed shut and his hands joined together as Mr Dawson's voice went up and down. At last there was a general sigh, backs settled against chairs, and, as Enoch opened his eyes, the grown-ups were opening their Bibles.

Mrs Liverstitch shifted him onto one side, and held hers one-handed.

'Where had we got to?' she demanded. 'We don't seem to be making much progress with this.'

Enoch wriggled uncomfortably. He knew this was directed at his mother, who had found so much to discuss and argue about that they had only reached the story of Cain and Abel after six meetings.

Ellen Kirk gave an offended sniff, and Mr Dawson intervened hastily.

'Genesis, chapter four. Shall I read?'

He read the chapter in a smooth light voice. Enoch squinted sideways at Mrs Liverstitch's Bible, trying to pick out some words. He knew Mrs Liverstitch couldn't really read, for she had told him. But when he grew up he would be a vicar like Mr Dawson, a clever man with a shiny white collar, and then he could teach Mrs Liverstitch just like Dan was teaching him.

When Mr Dawson finished reading he looked encouragingly around the group. 'Has anyone any thoughts they would like to share?'

Enoch stared at him in surprise. Didn't Mr Dawson know that Mr Spraggs never uttered a word? Hadn't he noticed that Mrs Liverstitch had just popped another peppermint into her mouth, and that Mam always waited for someone else to speak first so that she could contradict them?

Whatever Mr Dawson knew, he only waited a second before beginning himself.

'I think,' he began magisterially, 'the key to this story lies in verses four to seven. The Lord accepts Abel's offering and rejects Cain's, but not without a reason. Sin, my friends, has already corrupted the heart of Cain long before he contemplates the murder of his righteous and innocent brother.'

Enoch was watching his mother. He didn't understand the vicar's words, but he could see her restless disapproval.

'God rejects Cain and accepts Abel,' she interrupted. 'God judges, that's all we need to know. It's not for us to reason about his judgements.'

Then they were hard at it. Enoch could not follow the words, but he could follow the fight all right. His mother got Mr Dawson in her jaws and worried him like a terrier. Enoch could see the vicar looking first surprised, then anxious, then sulkily defeated.

'I think we shall begin the next chapter,' Mr Dawson announced shortly, and Mam sat back with a look of triumph.

Enoch snuggled up against Mrs Liverstitch, and her arms tightened round him. He was beginning to get sleepy. As Mr Dawson began to read in his high precise voice, Enoch closed his eyes. Names and numbers drifted over him. He thought he heard Daniel begin to play his trumpet very softly, so softly it was right inside his head. He slipped sideways on Mrs Liverstitch's lap and gave himself up to sleep.

Suddenly he was awake again. He had heard his name.

'*And all the days of Enoch were three hundred sixty and five years,*' announced Mr Dawson. '*And Enoch walked with God, and he was not; for God took him.*'

Enoch began to howl. He did not want to be taken away. He was happy here with Dan. If God took him, it would be to punish him. Mam had made that clear enough.

Mrs Liverstitch put up her fat arms to comfort him, but Enoch twisted away from her and fell off her lap on to the floor.

'I don't want it,' he sobbed. 'I don't want Him to!'

His mother pulled him to his feet and slapped him.

'Shut up, you little heathen!'

His voice rose to a pitch that made her desperate. She began to shake him.

'Shaming me! It's a pity you weren't taken when you were born!'

There was an appalled silence, broken only by the noise of Enoch's crying.

Her words were too familiar to have hurt him much, but the slapping and shaking on top of his fright had left him gulping in panic.

Mr Dawson got up and led Ellen gently back to her chair.

'Someone take the boy up to bed,' he said. 'He should never have been down here in the first place.'

Mrs Liverstitch gathered Enoch up into her arms. He clung to her, sobbing, as she carried him upstairs, murmuring comforts at every step. She undressed him and slipped him into bed, next to Daniel, sitting up anxiously in his clean nightshirt.

'What was all that yelling about?' Daniel demanded.

Mrs Liverstitch shook her head.

'Best ask your mother yourself,' she said. 'It's not for me to say, I'm sure.'

Before she left she bent over Enoch and kissed him on the lips. 'Poor mite,' she said. 'As if it was any fault of yours, anyhow.'

3

Daniel's lost dreams

Sleet was flicking against the grimy window of the back bedroom. It was Saturday, a half-day at the terracotta factory where their mother worked. Enoch lay hunched up under the bedclothes. He had scarcely spoken since breakfast time. Daniel reached over and touched him gently on the shoulder.

'She really let you have it last night, didn't she? I told her you'd only make a noise if you stayed up.'

Enoch curled himself into a tighter ball. It hurt him even to think about it. Why did Daniel keep trying to make him talk?

'It's only her temper,' Daniel went on. 'She doesn't mean anything by it. She used to shout at me when I was little, then she'd be sorry, and buy me sweets to make it up.'

Enoch gave an angry kick.

'She never gets me the sweets, though,' he said in a muffled voice.

'None of us get the sweets nowadays,' Daniel replied wryly. 'Cheer up, now. Why don't you sit up, and we can do some letters and numbers?'

Enoch said nothing, only wriggled further into his own corner of the bed. He knew Daniel was disappointed, but he felt too tired, too defeated to learn. Besides he was angry with his brother for not telling the truth. Didn't Daniel understand, or was he trying to make Enoch feel better? Mam did mean something by it. It wasn't only her temper. She meant it. She wished he was dead, and she didn't care who knew it.

He could feel Daniel leaning out of bed to rummage in the old tin trunk where he kept his things. He hoped he was getting out the scrapbook with the coloured pictures in, that Polly had made for Dan when they were both little. Enoch liked to look at that and hear Daniel talk. But to his dismay, it was the Bible Daniel was getting.

He felt a sharp dig in his ribs as Daniel began to read aloud.

'Listen, Enoch, this'll stir you up a bit.'

Enoch put his hands over his ears, determined to not to listen to the frightening words. He knew why Daniel was doing it. He couldn't stand it when Enoch refused to do lessons with him. Teaching meant much more than a way of passing the time to Daniel. He had always wanted to be a teacher. But there had been no money for him to stay on at school. Now when he was teaching Enoch he could escape back into his dreams.

Daniel read on. '*And they shall go into the holes of the rocks, and into the caves of the earth, for fear of the Lord, and for the glory of his majesty, when he ariseth to shake terribly the earth.*'

Enoch couldn't stand it any longer. His head came up out of the bedclothes like an outraged jack-in-the-box.

'Don't,' he said. 'Don't, Dan, it's horrible.'

'It's the Word of the Lord,' Daniel said with terrifying calm.

Enoch clenched his fists.

'Shut up,' he said desperately. 'Shut up, now!'

Dan's face suddenly softened.

'Oh, come on, you little rabbit,' he said, pulling him over onto his lap. 'You scare easy, don't you? I like all that blood and thunder stuff. But that was in the old days in the time before Our Saviour. It's over and done with, see?'

'Really over?' Enoch demanded. He snuggled up to

Dan, liking the feel of his brother's warm arms around him.

'Really over,' said Dan. 'Don't let Mam make you think otherwise.'

His stomach rumbled noisily, making them both laugh. Then Daniel reached across to the little table for his slate.

'Come on, let's practise your writing. That last bit you did for me was really good.'

But Enoch wanted to talk instead. 'When I grow up will I be rich or poor?'

Daniel looked at him in surprise. 'Why are you asking me that?'

Enoch fingered the ragged coverlet. 'I just thought if I knew I was going to be rich I could tell Mam, and she might like me a bit more, that's all.'

Daniel hugged him tightly. 'Never mind Mam,' he said. 'You've got me, all right?'

Enoch nodded. It was hard not to mind about Mam, though. He couldn't help thinking how different she sounded in the stories Daniel told him of the old days. She had brought sweets home and kissed Daniel and the baby goodnight. Perhaps in those days Mam would have liked him too.

'Why are we so poor, Daniel?' he persisted. 'I don't like it.'

Daniel made a wry face. 'I don't, either. But there's only Mam to earn money now, and they don't pay women very much. That's why, when Dad died, and my legs got hurt, Mam had to send away Louisa and Stephen.'

'Louisa went into service,' said Enoch. 'And then she died. That's right, isn't it?'

Daniel nodded. 'Scarlet fever. Poor Louisa. She was a skinny little thing, but full of mischief.'

'And Stephen went to Auntie Irene's, and I stayed here with you.'

Daniel gave him a squeeze. 'And a good job you did, or what would I do all day?'

Enoch grinned with pleasure. Daniel's closeness gave him the courage to ask again the question his brother would never answer.

'So where does Polly come into it?'

Daniel's face closed up. 'She doesn't, not any more.'

He took his arm away, and got the slate again, rubbing it clean with his sleeve.

'No more idle talk. Time for a bit of work,' he said firmly.

Reluctantly, Enoch sat up straight, and took the slate and the pencil from Daniel.

'She is my sister, though, isn't she? You said she was the eldest.'

'Well, if I said that, it must be true, mustn't it?'

'And where is she working?'

Daniel hesitated, then shook his head.

'Mam won't have me talking to you about Polly, Enoch, so that's that. Good try, though.' He gave his brother a gentle pat on the arm. 'Now come on. Write your name out for me, and then we'll try some easy words.'

'I see her sometimes,' Enoch blurted out. 'Daniel, sometimes I see Polly, outside on the street.'

There was a silence. Then:

'I guessed you did,' said Daniel. 'She gave you that toy you keep under your pillow, didn't she?'

Enoch nodded. He was actually holding it in his hand under the bedclothes. It was a small mouse made out of old grey flannel, with buttons for eyes, and a tail of wool.

'I told Mam it came from Mrs Liverstitch,' said Daniel. 'She found it last time she came to change the bed.'

Enoch's eyes opened wide. 'But that was a lie, Daniel!'

Daniel grinned. 'Well, perhaps I said it must be from Mrs Liverstitch, because who else would give it you?'

Enoch put the mouse carefully inside his shirt. 'I

won't leave it in the bed any more,' he said.

Daniel looked sideways at Enoch.

'When you next see Polly, will you give her my love?' he said in an odd quick way. 'Tell her how I'm looking after you. She'll be happy about that. I never thought it was right of Mam to –' he broke off and looked confused.

'What, Daniel?' Enoch demanded eagerly. 'Not right of Mam to what?'

But Daniel only shook his head, and began, maddeningly, to whistle.

4

Polly's promise

Enoch sat under the kitchen table, hugging the leg of a chair and listening to his mother and Mrs Liverstitch.

'It's for the best, Ellen,' Mrs Liverstitch said, finishing her second cup of tea.

'He's not gone yet.' Ellen Kirk spoke in a low passionate voice. 'He might pull through.'

Mrs Liverstitch made a sad noise as if she doubted it.

'He was the strongest of them all,' Ellen said. 'He was born in that bed. My first boy. He was so red with yelling when they put him in my arms –' Her voice stopped, and her hands covered her eyes.

Enoch, craning up at her, could see the tears escaping between her fingers. It scared him to see her crying over Dan. It scared him more than not being allowed in the bedroom any more. Mrs Liverstitch had explained that yesterday: Dan needed to rest, and it was only the fever that made him make those noises. It was good Mrs Liverstitch came, because Mam explained nothing.

'Still, you're paid up with the funeral club,' she said to Mam in a comforting tone. 'You've had the doctor for him. You'll have the means to bury him, if it comes to it.'

'But it's more than I can bear,' Ellen Kirk whispered. 'He's been a rock to me, Annie. When his father was killed in the pit, I thought I would go out of my mind. It seemed like a miracle when they brought Dan out. Then there was Enoch. Without Dan, God knows what would have happened to him. The workhouse, maybe.'

'Heaven forbid!' exclaimed Mrs Liverstitch.

She reached for Enoch's hand under the table, but he shied away from her. Daniel was the one he needed to explain all this strange talk, but it was Daniel he couldn't have.

'And not a penny from the old man. His own grandchildren, and he let them go about shoeless in winter.'

'It's a shame,' Mrs Liverstitch agreed. 'I suppose it

all goes to your husband's brother, the son he lives with.'

Enoch saw his mother draw herself up, wiping her face on the back of her hand.

'We managed,' she said, not without pride. 'I suppose I'll go on managing. But there is something you could do for me, if you have a mind.'

'Of course.' Mrs Liverstitch nodded eagerly. 'Whatever I can do to help, Ellen, you know that.'

'I was thinking you might take Enoch, just for the day. He's been such a nuisance, trying to get in to see Daniel, and making a noise. I've had to take him into my bed, so of course he's started wetting.'

She called out to Enoch with sudden venom. 'If you do it again tonight, I'm going to rub your face in it, do you hear?'

'Yes, Mam,' Enoch said sullenly. He put his hands over his ears to block out anything else she might say to him. He let his hands off slowly – off, on, off, on – so that their words were distorted into a crashing jumble like the noise of the mill machines at night. He wouldn't care about anything they said. He wouldn't listen to anything until he was safely back with Daniel.

Suddenly Mrs Liverstitch's face appeared next to him like a great round moon under the table. She was bending down to peer at him and smiling kindly.

'Would you like to come to my house now, poppet?' she asked.

Enoch said nothing. He didn't want to leave Daniel, but he didn't want to hurt Mrs Liverstitch's feelings either.

'He'll like it,' said his mother. 'Just you let me know if he doesn't.'

Mrs Liverstitch took him home with her, and taught him how to play snap. They laughed when he kept winning. Enoch found it strange that he could enjoy himself with Dan so ill, but he did. He was glad when Mrs Liverstitch came to fetch him again next morning. When they got to her house she sat him down and gave him black sugary tea with bread sopped in it. Enoch ate hungrily, looking round. The kitchen was not very clean, nor was it very tidy. He asked Mrs Liverstitch why it was like that. She looked surprised at first, then she laughed.

'I suppose I've always found a sit-down more attractive than a clean-up! But never mind a bit of dirt, Enoch. Look at all the nice things.'

There were indeed lots of interesting things Enoch would like to touch and handle. A collection of rather dusty ornate paper fans were arranged on the mantelpiece, and there was a vase full of big feathery grasses on the floor by the range. The dresser had a shelf of coloured glasses and little painted stones and other ornaments. They were souvenirs, Mrs Liverstitch said, brought back from Matlock by her sister-in-law who used go every year.

'Every year, for a whole week,' said Mrs Liverstitch. 'Can you imagine? Her husband did very well for himself. He was a colliery clerk, with money left him by his uncle. Not that it did them any good in the end. Died of black fever in 1870, along with many more poor souls.'

'Is that what Daniel's got?'

Mrs Liverstitch shook her head.

'He's got pneumonia, the doctor thinks.'

Enoch stirred the spoon round and round his teacup, not looking up.

'Will Daniel be all right?' he asked softly.

Mrs Liverstitch put her big hand over his small one.

'We are being gloomy this morning, aren't we, the pair of us?' she said in a voice that tried to be jolly, but came out all wrong.

She patted his hand, then heaved herself up out of her chair.

'I have to get on,' she said briskly. 'I turn out the lodgers' room once a week, not that they notice, being men. If you're a good boy while I'm upstairs, you can walk to the shop with me later. You be careful of old Stripe, now,' she added, pointing to the large ginger tabby cat basking on the hearth-rug. 'And don't fetch anything down off the shelves or poke about in the cupboards, or you'll break something. That won't be a nice thing to have to go home and tell your mam, will it?'

Enoch's fingers darted to the safety of his armpits.

'I won't touch a thing,' he promised earnestly.

'Good lad.'

He watched her disappear up the stairs, then slid down from his chair and went slowly around the room. She had a black shiny sofa against one wall. Next to it was the dresser, which had a glass-fronted cupboard. There were plates and bowls inside it, all sizes, but with the same lovely orange and pink and gold pattern. He got down on his knees and pressed his face against the glass, rubbing again and again as his breath misted it up. He was hungry for the colours. They were such lovely plates, too lovely to put grey lumpy porridge or bread on. She had a blood-red geranium in a pot on her windowsill and a picture on the wall of a little girl with a basket of flowers. It was much nicer than Mam's house. If Daniel did not get better, he wondered if he could come and live here and not be left alone with Mam.

From upstairs came the noise of a broom knocking against walls. Enoch wished Mrs Liverstitch would come downstairs again. There really wasn't much he could do by himself if he wasn't to touch anything, except maybe stroke the cat. He walked over to the hearth. Stripe's ears were ragged and his nose scarred with fighting, but he allowed Enoch to run his hands down his hot fur from his shoulder blades to the base of his tail, though the tip flicked as a warning not to take liberties. Enoch marvelled that Stripe could be so hot and not feel it. He was painful to touch.

'Coal-hot, stove-hot,' he murmured, scratching the cat behind the ears. 'Will you play with me?'

But Stripe was too lazy to stir.

Enoch was getting up to look for a bit of string when there was a knock at the scullery door, so soft he wasn't sure at first that he had heard it. He stood looking, wondering whether to fetch Mrs Liverstitch.

Then the door opened.

'Enoch!' gasped his sister Polly. 'I didn't know Annie was looking after you! I came to ask about Daniel.'

Enoch didn't answer her. He felt shy and strange. It was so long since he had seen her. He looked away along the floor and rubbed his bare feet together.

'You've grown,' she said. 'Come on, let me look at you.'

She grabbed his arms and swung him up, laughing as if just the look of him made her happy. Suddenly it was all right again. Enoch started laughing too, and they were looking and hugging, and his arms were lost in the deep warm inside of her shawl.

'I haven't seen you for so long,' she said. 'And I can only stay a minute. I don't live in Gresley any more, Enoch. That's why you haven't seen me. I'm working for a family in Burton now. It's taken me more than an hour to walk over.'

He held her tight, the stiff cotton of her apron feeling cool against his cheek. Then he took hold of her fingers, opening and shutting them gently. He needed to press her into his memory.

She lifted him up and carried him over to a chair. She took him on her lap, murmuring about how thin he was. He snuggled right up with his face against her neck and his fingers in her hair, re-learning the smell and feel of her.

'And have they been looking after you at home, love? Is Mam treating you all right?'

He didn't know what to say about that. But he remembered about Daniel, what Daniel had asked him to tell her.

'Daniel's looking after me, Polly,' he said proudly. 'He's teaching me to read and everything. He said to give you his love.'

Polly gave him a squeeze.

'That means a lot to me,' she said, her eyes shining. 'You know, Enoch, I haven't seen him since you were a baby. I wish I could see him now.'

There was a great clatter and panting on the stairs, and Mrs Liverstitch was down in the room.

'Enoch, why didn't you shout up to me that Polly was here?' she cried. She looked at them cuddled together as if she didn't know whether to smile or cry.

'Enoch,' said Polly quickly, 'Mam doesn't know that I come and see Mrs Liverstitch sometimes. It's a kind of secret. You needn't tell any lies, but you don't have to tell Mam anything about it, understand?'

Enoch nodded. He certainly understood about not telling things to Mam.

Then Polly jumped up and Mrs Liverstitch began talking to her in a low murmur, though not so low that Enoch couldn't hear it.

'She told me he was even worse this morning. A neighbour's sitting with him now, and she's going to come home at dinner-time herself.'

Enoch gave a low stricken cry. He wanted Daniel. He had forgotten how much he wanted Daniel. Polly held out her arms to pick him up, but he ducked round the back of her and ran for the door.

Once out on the street he stood for a moment, perplexed, as he looked to right and left and saw the houses march identically away. But a few yards down the alley he spotted a landmark, some scrawny weeds sprouting up where a cobble was missing.

He was about to set off at a run, when he heard Polly come after him. She put her hand on his shoulder gently, not restraining him, but saying goodbye.

'Enoch, I can't come to see Daniel. Mam won't let me. But I'll be back for you, I promise. Burton's not so far. I'll come when I can.'

He looked up. She was smiling, but her eyes were so sad. He was reaching for her hand, when Mrs Liverstitch suddenly popped up on the other side of him. 'Got you, you young varmint,' she said breathlessly.

Enoch let out a shriek of laughter, and the chase was on. He was off down the road as fast as he could. Mrs Liverstitch began to trot after him, muttering and waving. But Enoch could already see the main road, and when he had crossed to the corner, he could see his own street. He looked back, and there was Mrs Liverstitch, too old and fat and breathless ever to catch him up. Laughing with the pleasure of it, he raced to his own back doorstep, and only then did he remember why he had come.

There was no one in the kitchen. A red knitted shawl hung over the back of one of the chairs, and Mr Dawson's hat was on the table. Enoch crept upstairs, afraid of the silence. The bedroom door was closed, but now at last he could hear them. His mother was sobbing. Mr Dawson's voice, shaken but controlled, was reading an unfamiliar prayer. The bedsprings were squeaking as if Daniel was thrashing about, as if he was trying to get up. Suddenly his voice came, beginning in a deep grunt and ending in a shriek.

'No, no, no!'

It cut through Mr Dawson's prayer, but he carried on almost without a pause. Then came another deep shout that was almost a bark, as if Daniel's mouth had been taken over by an animal. With a cry of pity, Enoch tore at the door and rushed into the room, past his mother and the neighbour. He ran right up to the bed where Daniel was twisting and groaning, and dived under it, fetching up the slate and the Bible.

'It's all right, Daniel,' he shouted. 'Here are your things. You can read to me, or we can do some sums, I don't mind which.'

It had always calmed him. It had always brought him out of his queer mood. But this time one of

Daniel's arms struck out and the things were swept out of Enoch's grasp. The Bible hit the wall, crushing its fragile pages, and the slate fell out of its frame on to the floor and broke into three pieces.

Enoch picked up the pieces and held them tightly.

'I saw Polly,' he said. 'I told her what you asked me. She wanted to come and see you, Dan, but she couldn't. Please don't mind that she couldn't, Dan. I don't understand about it, but Mam could tell you.'

Tears were running down his face now, but Daniel didn't seem to know it. Mam pulled him away, and shouted questions about Polly, but he didn't care about her red angry face and her iron hands. He wouldn't tell her anything, no matter how she hurt him. Suddenly black cloth arms were round him, and Mr Dawson's fob watch was pressing against the back of his head. Mr Dawson was speaking in a tight shocked voice:

'A deathbed is no place for this – this cruelty, Mrs Kirk. Let the child alone.'

Enoch saw the look of shock and anger on his mother's face. He felt frightened for Mr Dawson.

Then Mrs Liverstitch waddled into the bedroom, wheezing complaints and apologies. She took Enoch from Mr Dawson and marched him downstairs. She would not let go of him when they reached the kitchen. Even when he had to go to the privy, she escorted him across the yard and stood outside the door, grumbling.

'Rushing in like that, and interrupting Mr Dawson in his prayers. Shouting and yelling about sums, as if your brother could give you lessons, the condition he's in. And all that talk about Polly. You'll get me into trouble, you will. Why go upsetting your mother with all that, as if she hasn't got enough to cry about? It's enough to break a person's heart, what's happened in this family.'

Enoch wasn't listening. He was thinking about Daniel. It came to him in that tight stinking place, that his brother was dying: not like a Christian, but in one of his queer rages. A slow fear started to wind round Enoch's legs, up into his stomach and his lungs until it pressed his whole body so hard he could hardly breathe. Daniel had cried out against Mr Dawson's praying. He had sounded like a devil, screaming and shouting. It was as though God had hardened Daniel's heart. And what would happen to Enoch now, with only Mam to look after him?

'Enoch, lad, come on now, and open the door. Enoch, I won't be cross with you.'

The anger had left Mrs Liverstitch's voice and a note of fear had crept in. She began to thump gently on the door and peer in at the crack. But Enoch had forgotten she was there. His hand crept into his shirt and closed on the little grey mouse. Polly had promised she would come back.

5

Leaving home

Enoch stood in the bedroom. He hugged himself and rocked anxiously as he watched his mother opening drawers and collecting his things. She had a comb, his other shirt and his Sunday trousers. There were some stockings that had been Daniel's. She felt under the pillow for the rag of a jersey Enoch used as a nightshirt, and then stooped to drag it out from under the bed with a grimace. She was off downstairs with her arms full, while he trailed after her, repeating the question:

'Where are we going?'

She spilled the things onto the table before replying. 'We're not. You are.'

She fetched a sheet of newspaper and a bit of string from the dresser and started to make a parcel of the clothes. Enoch said nothing, watching helplessly until she beckoned him to put his finger on the taut string so she could knot it.

'You're going to your uncle's, to Uncle Stephen's.'

Enoch tried to isolate Uncle Stephen from the mass of dark-coated men at Daniel's funeral.

'I don't want to go. Why can't I stay here?'

'Because I have to work, and there's no one to look after you.'

'I can look after myself.'

'Don't be so daft!' His mother retorted scornfully. 'You're too young for school and I don't trust you on your own inside this house all day.'

'I'll stay outside then. I don't mind.'

'No, but I do. I didn't ask to have you. It's someone else's turn to bear the burden.'

Enoch's fingers gripped the edge of the table. He was scared now. He didn't want to be with Mam, but he had to stay at home. Polly had promised to come for him. How could she, if he wasn't here? He had last seen her outside the church after the funeral. She was standing a little apart from the other mourners, her face blotched and wet with crying. When he tried to run to her, Mam had yanked him back so hard his arm had ached for days.

'Does Polly know I'm going?' he dared to ask.

Mam stared at him harshly. 'Not that I know of.'

'Please tell her, Mam,' he whispered. 'Please tell her where I'm going.'

'I won't be seeing her,' Mam said. Her manner was a knife's edge away from violence. 'And find your cap now. I haven't got all day.'

But it was she who had to find his cap and pick up the parcel and, finally, prise him away from the table. He let her drag him as far as the street and then he lay down on the cobbles with his face to the wet stones. A gang of children stopped their game to watch as his mother picked him up by the collar and set him on his feet, clouting him hard on the back. Enoch abandoned himself to screaming and flung himself down in the road again. Now the women came to the doors to see as his mother, crying with rage and humiliation, tried to pull him up by the hair. Then a dog set upon the parcel she had dropped and worried it into a muddy puddle. As Ellen Kirk's screams rose to a pitch of desperation, Mr Dawson appeared at the corner of the street.

'He's too much for me, Mr Dawson, too much for any woman on her own. The devil's in that child and I haven't the strength to beat him out.'

Mr Dawson was shocked. He swallowed hard, then asked:

'Where were you trying to take him?'

'To his uncle's. To Townsend Farm.'

Mr Dawson looked down at Enoch. He was crouching in the mud, his head well down, defended by his elbows and knees.

'I'll take him,' he said quietly.

Ellen Kirk nodded. The rage went out of her, and left her empty and exhausted.

'Goodbye, Enoch,' she said.

He didn't lift his head.

She turned for home, walking almost blindly past the whispering neighbours and the children chanting their rhymes.

As soon as she had gone Mr Dawson picked Enoch up and set him on his feet. He retrieved the muddied clothes and tied them into a bundle. He slung this from the hook of his umbrella and offered it to Enoch to carry over his shoulder.

'Off to seek your fortune like Dick Whittington, eh?' he said gaily.

Enoch knew when he was beaten. He let Mr Dawson lead him away without protest.

They tramped down the long street under a grey January sky thickened by factory smoke. After a time they left the town behind them and took the road, which skirted Gresley Common. The ground was rough, covered in low bushes, coarse grass and bracken, cut back here and there to expose deep pits of reddish clay. Enoch was unsettled by the openness of it. There were fields one side and the common the other, and the road was churned to muddy porridge in between. The drizzle thickened into rain, and Mr Dawson made Enoch carry the bundle so that he could use his umbrella. The boy clutched the sodden burden and struggled through the mud, trying to keep pace with Mr Dawson's brisk stride. Once or twice he stumbled, and felt Mr Dawson's steadying hand on his back.

At last it seemed to Enoch that they had always been walking through the freezing rain. There was only the ache in his legs and the cold drip of rain down his neck where the umbrella didn't cover him. It did not even seem as if they was moving, for the rain was now so heavy he could barely see. Then suddenly Mr Dawson stopped at a gate. He put his hand on Enoch's shoulder, and they went in together.

In the yard there was the barking of a chained and angry dog, and then over it the scolding voice of a woman. She appeared, running towards them with a shawl over her head. There was an exchange between the woman and Mr Dawson. Enoch caught only part of it, something about the weather and the Kirks having a cart at their disposal. Mr Dawson sounded angry. The woman stooped to look at Enoch. Her face was not unpleasant, soft and plump, but deeply lined. Then she was talking to Mr Dawson, urging him to at least come in and dry himself by the fire.

Mr Dawson led Enoch inside and took the bundle from him.

'Is that all he's got with him?' the woman said in dismay. 'It's all over mud as well.'

'There was an accident,' said Mr Dawson. He fiddled with his hat for a minute, then put it back on.

'Mr Kirk won't be back until suppertime.' The woman looked vaguely round at the kettle. 'You don't need to be going straight away.'

But Mr Dawson had no wish to stay. He picked up his dripping umbrella and laid his hand on Enoch's rain-plastered hair with unexpected gentleness.

'Be a good boy and say your prayers. You'll soon settle in here, I'm sure. And I expect your mother will be along to visit you. We don't want her to hear any tales of naughtiness, do we?'

Miserably, Enoch shook his head. As Mr Dawson removed his hand Enoch twisted round and clutched it in both of his.

'Tell her I'm a good boy really,' he gabbled. 'Tell her to have me back.'

Dismayed, Mr Dawson freed himself with a murmur of reassurance and made for the door. Then he was gone, and the woman with him, and Enoch was alone in the big shadowy room. He heard the dog barking outside as Mr Dawson crossed the yard. He listened intently, not daring to lift his eyes to look at the things around him. He felt an urge to wet himself. Then there was a noise above his head, a groaning of boards and footsteps on the stairs. The tread was heavy and deliberate. Enoch's fear grew. The noise changed as it reached the tiled floor of the kitchen. Enoch turned, trembling. Someone was standing near him. He saw slippers, black trousers, broad black coat and a neck rising, red and corded, from the shiny white collar. He got no further. With a rush, arms were round him and he heard through his tears an old voice murmuring nonsense words, any words, words of comfort.

When he looked at last at the face, bright old eyes met his with love.

'Welcome, my little grandson!'

PART TWO

'Fancy having a brother and
not knowing!'

6

At the farm

'You've been with us for two weeks already,' Grandad whispered to Enoch as they sat down together at the table. 'I can hardly believe how the days fly past.'

Enoch took the old man's hand under the table. He liked to have the comfort of it, especially when the family came together at meals. It was strange here, so different from Mam's house. Yet when he thought of himself at home, it already seemed a far off time, like a story in a book.

The kitchen table at the farmhouse was covered in a blue checked cloth and a brass oil lamp hung over it, casting a circle of light over the plates and dishes. As Auntie May set down a bowl of steaming white potatoes and a dish of greens, Uncle Stephen, frowning with concentration, began to carve the mutton. He was a big man, his face, though still handsome, running to fat and broken veins. He sent the large blue and white plates along the table loaded with glistening meat. Enoch's mouth watered when his plate came, but he had learned that you didn't start eating straight away. You put all the things on your plate and ate them all together. When it was his turn for the potatoes, Grandad helped him topple two on to his plate with the big spoon. Opposite him his cousins, Harold and Edy, were stirring their cabbage gingerly, trying to hide bits of meat under it. It amazed Enoch, the faces they pulled at the sight of a lovely dinner.

Uncle Stephen cleared his throat.

'Rain's set in again tonight, I notice.'

It was a bit like grace, Enoch thought, only grace was never said here. Sometimes Uncle Stephen spoke before they were settled in their seats. Sometimes, if his day had gone badly, he did not speak at all. But only after Uncle Stephen spoke was anyone else supposed to.

Enoch's cousin Edy at once raised her high aggrieved voice, addressing her mother across the table.

'I'm not speaking to Alice Brady any more, Mam. Do you know what she called me?'

Enoch listened in awe. She made school sound

such an exciting place. Her feuds and friendships shifted so rapidly that he could never keep up. He liked Edy, though she mostly ignored him. She was twelve years old, a big lump of a girl with a moon face and long thin brown hair that resisted all efforts with the curling irons.

'And didn't Sarah do anything to help?' Auntie May asked hopefully as Edy paused to draw breath.

'Oh, Mam!' Edy was disgusted. 'I told you last week. Sarah's gone off with Mary Prickett and won't speak to me any more.'

Harold cut across his sister's story in his clear treble.

'How are my old boots suiting you, Enoch? Better than the pair you arrived in, aren't they?'

Edy sniggered and then caught her grandfather's eye. She turned a slow red.

'Shut up, Harold, I was talking,' she muttered.

Enoch felt Grandad give his hand a squeeze under the table. But he didn't care about the teasing, not much anyway. Harold didn't know how to share anything, not even an old pair of boots. That was how Grandad had explained it.

There had been such a big fuss about his clothes when he arrived. Auntie May had burnt the lot, not even bothered to wash them, and sorted out some old clothes of Harold's for him to wear. His boots, like his mother's black coat, had come from the pawnshop in exchange for Daniel's trumpet. But Auntie May had turned them over and seen the holes, and pulled out the paper his mother had stuffed in to make them fit, and her face had gone peculiar.

'Don't be unkind, Harold,' said his mother now. 'Are you going to bother Enoch about your boots every night until he goes home?'

Harold looked sullen and kicked the table leg. Uncle Stephen came to his defence at once.

'Harold is not being unkind, May. There's no harm in keeping the realities of the situation in view. It's the first time in my life I've been asked to take on a charity case, especially one whose origins are, shall we say, a little dubious. I still don't quite know how you talked me into it.'

'We were very happy to have Enoch,' Auntie May said. Her voice was loud and bright, and she gave a little nod, trying to indicate with her eyes that Enoch was listening.

But Uncle Stephen met Enoch's gaze and went on talking.

'I've no doubt some of us were. But I didn't expect to have to clothe him and shoe him as well as feed him. I saw what that woman sent him with, and it would have disgraced the workhouse.'

60

'Poverty is no disgrace,' said Enoch's grandfather in his slow, rather deep voice. 'Unless, of course, it is brought about by mismanagement or self-indulgence, Stephen.'

Enoch looked from one to the other. Grandad had made Uncle Stephen angry, but strangely, Uncle Stephen only opened his second bottle of beer with a snort.

'Well, Enoch and I had a pleasant day of it,' the old man continued after a moment, patting the boy's hand. 'We walked down to the bottom field and watched the men ploughing, and then we took the dogs for a run across the common.'

'And Enoch helped Nellie and me with the dinner,' Auntie May put in. 'He laid the table all by himself, the clever little thing.'

She got up to go into the kitchen, where Nellie, the young maid of all work, was dishing up the steamed pudding. Nellie always made him think of Polly, working for a family in Burton. He wondered if Polly had been back to Gresley yet. Would she look for him in the streets? Would she dare to ask Mam where he was, and what would Mam say if she did? It gnawed at him, the feeling that Polly might be looking for him. But there was no one he dared ask, not even Grandad. Stealthily, he put his hand up to his shirt and felt the warm soft bump that was his little cloth mouse. While he had it, he felt as if he was still close to Polly.

Harold started in on Enoch again.

'I saw Stephen today, Enoch. I went into Gresley after school, and there he was, out playing in your old street.'

'Who's Stephen?' Enoch asked warily.

'He's your brother, Enoch,' Auntie May said with a slight frown of surprise. 'Don't you remember him?'

'Fancy having a brother and not knowing!' Edy screamed in derision.

'Of course I know about Stephen,' Enoch said crossly. 'He lives in Ashby with Auntie Irene.'

Auntie May frowned.

'Not now, he doesn't, Enoch dear. He's gone back home to live with your mother.'

Enoch put his hands up to his ears, but he let the sounds come in. He didn't want to hear, but he had to. He had to know.

'Why can Stephen be at home, when I got sent here?' he asked.

'That's what we'd all like to know,' muttered Uncle Stephen.

Auntie May frowned. 'Auntie Irene's got two little ones of her own and her husband's not very well, so when she heard Enoch was coming to us Stephen got sent home again.'

She reached out to smooth the worry lines on Enoch's face.

'He's older than you are, Enoch. Stephen can manage on his own while your Mam's at work. And he's ever such a nice boy, isn't he, Harold? I expect he'll be at Woodville School when you start. Your Mam was telling me he hasn't been to school yet, for all he's nearly seven. So he'll be put in the beginners' standard, same as you.' She laughed. 'You'll get the teacher all mixed up. You're as like as two peas, with you being so big for your age.'

Enoch pushed his plate across the table in sudden fury.

'I don't want this,' he said. 'It tastes horrible.'

Auntie May was visibly upset. But before she could speak, Harold got in first.

'Stephen's got a top. He showed it me today. His mam gave him it when he came home, he said. She was that pleased –'

'Harold!' interrupted his grandfather sharply. 'Don't talk with your mouth full of food.'

'I'll correct the manners of my son, if you please,' Uncle Stephen barked. 'He's got a right to talk at this table. He belongs to this family, one hundred per cent,

which is more than you can say for that little object.'
He jerked his head over at Enoch.

Harold smirked, and stuck out his tongue. Under the table, Grandad squeezed Enoch's hand so tight it hurt.

'Shall we go and have a story in the front parlour?' Enoch whispered.

It puzzled him that no one else in the family wanted to be with Grandad, to hear his stories and to play with him. It didn't matter what he was talking about, Harold and Edy never listened, they just looked bored. Uncle Stephen was so impatient, and Auntie May so busy. Grandad was like him, not really wanted. But Enoch loved to be with him. He reminded Enoch of Daniel, he loved books so much. But Grandad never talked about Daniel, so Enoch didn't either, just as he didn't ever mention Polly. When he was with Daniel, Enoch had thought there was only the Bible and schoolbooks, but Grandad had some lovely red and gold books by a man called Walter Scott. The stories lived in Enoch's head for days. He acted them out on their walks and talked them over with Grandad endlessly.

He was hoping for *Ivanhoe* tonight, and was deeply disappointed when Grandad shook his head.

'I can't bear it in there with no fire tonight,' he said in a low voice. 'My legs are aching as it is.'

He eased himself to his feet.

'I think I will go to bed now, May,' he said out loud. 'My joints are quite stiff and it's a damp night.'

Uncle Stephen gave a short bark of sarcastic laughter.

'The Almighty won't find you on your knees tonight, then, Dad?'

'One doesn't have to kneel in order to pray,' the old man replied. He beckoned to Enoch to come. But Enoch shook his head emphatically. Grandad only read the Bible in bed and he wanted *Ivanhoe*. His grandfather smiled, kissed him on the forehead and went upstairs alone.

Nellie came to clear the table, and Edy and her mother got out some mending. Uncle Stephen went to read his newspaper by the fire. Harold fetched out his box of soldiers and paraded them along the hearth-rug. Everyone had to be quiet while Uncle Stephen read his newspaper, so Harold's mouth moved silently with the sounds of battle, the trumpets and the guns.

Enoch laced his fingers together, mouthing a rhyme Daniel once taught him. 'Here is a church and here is a steeple . . .'

Uncle Stephen never read the Bible. Uncle Stephen never went to church. Neither Edy nor Harold had been baptised, and it was a great comfort to Enoch to know that if they died suddenly, they would surely go to Hell. Grandad was the only believer. On Enoch's first Sunday at the farm he had taken him to the communion service at Gresley. But it scared Enoch to see Mr Dawson in the pulpit, and his mother sitting in the third row from the back as if nothing was different. Back at the farm, Enoch blurted out to Auntie May that he did not want to go to church any more. Uncle Stephen smiled.

'Out of the mouths of babes, eh? This new generation will break the shackles of religion, you'll see, May. It's progress.'

Grandad went alone to church after that. Enoch was scared of what Mam would say when she found out he wasn't going any more. She would beat those Sundays back into him if she got the chance. But Grandad went on loving him, church or no church. God was more broadminded than Mam, Grandad said. And cuddled up on Grandad's lap, Enoch felt safe enough to believe it.

Bored with sitting alone, Enoch slid off his chair and went over to the hearth-rug. He had no toys of his own, and he was interested to see what Harold did with his. Harold, lying on his stomach to view his parade of soldiers, turned his head and scowled over his shoulder. 'What do you want?'

'I'm only looking.'

Enoch edged a bit closer and sat down on the corner of the rug.

'You can't look,' said Harold. 'I never said you could, and now I'm telling you, you can't.'

Enoch waited, and then sneaked a hand round one of the nearest soldiers when he thought Harold wasn't looking. With a shout of indignation, Harold snatched it off him, and gave Enoch a push. 'Is it my fault you've only got a stupid cloth mouse to play with? If you don't leave my things alone, I'll get it off you and throw it in the fire!'

Rage took Enoch by surprise. He lunged at Harold, pushing him up against the fireguard with all his might. He wanted Harold to go into the fire, to be burnt to pieces. Harold yelled and shoved back, scattering soldiers all over the hearth.

Down came Uncle Stephen's newspaper.

He picked up Enoch bodily, smacked him soundly, and pushed him up the dark stairs to find his own way to bed.

'You'll be back home with your mother if you keep this up, lad!' he shouted after him.

Enoch stood on the landing, breathing hard and crying just a little. He was shocked at what had just happened, frightened by the violence inside him. He waited without moving until they were quiet again downstairs. He wondered what to do. It was too early to go sleep. He didn't want to go into Grandad's room. Grandad would ask him what had happened, and he didn't know himself, except that it was about Polly. What if when he said Polly's name, Grandad's face took on that stiff disapproving look like Mam's? What was it that Polly had done? Enoch stood in the dark, and shivered. Did Mam think the devil was in Polly as well as him?

Instead he crept across the landing to his uncle and aunt's room. He knew where the candle and matches were kept. After some groping in the dark he found them and struck a light. He went over to the dressing table. There was the gilt-backed brush his aunt used for her own and Edy's hair. There was a bottle of lavender water, a scattering of hairpins, a ring tree and a pin-cushion whose tightly packed heads spelt 'Home, Sweet Home'. But what he had really come for was Auntie May's looking glass. Enoch held up the candle and stared at himself in the mirror until the milk-white face began to frighten him. As like as two peas, Auntie May had said. Stephen was a good boy, and Mam had taken him back. But he was here.

'Am I really the bad boy Mam says I am? What's wrong with me?'

7

Crimes and punishments

Enoch was standing with his face to the darkest corner of the room when Uncle Stephen came in for his midday dinner. Edy and Harold were at school, so the room was silent until Auntie May spoke.

'The devil's in that child today.'

Enoch heard his uncle grunt, and go on wiping the heavy mud off his boots. Then Uncle Stephen sat down at the table and Auntie May began serving. From his corner, Enoch heard the rich, ham-scented soup being ladled into bowls, then the clashing of spoons. Nobody spoke. The chairs creaked, the bread knife sawed, and Uncle Stephen sucked noisily. Saliva poured into Enoch's mouth, and his stomach started to clamour. But he knew there would be no chance of anything to eat today.

A chair scraped back upon the tiles.

'I'll just tell Nellie to take a tray up to your father,' said Auntie May. 'He went back to bed after his breakfast. The damp was affecting his joints that bad.'

She went out to the scullery and returned. Nellie's slipshod feet scuffed up the stairs, and then for what seemed an endless time, Enoch stood listening to the clock and to his own breathing. In a strange way he felt quite safe. He didn't really mind the waiting. He knew nothing would happen until Uncle Stephen was quite ready.

At last, Uncle Stephen said:

'So what has the nasty little beggar done this time?'

Enoch's heart began beating hard against his chest. He had been strapped for tampering with Auntie May's jewellery box. He had been strapped for breaking Harold's clockwork monkey. He had been strapped until he bled for stealing the egg money out of the purse kept on top of the dresser. This time he knew it would be even worse.

Auntie May's voice sounded as if she was close to tears. 'He broke my Crown Derby. All my lovely plates, Stephen!'

Uncle Stephen was already getting to his feet. Enoch heard him pulling off his belt.

'Come here you, and take hold of that chair.'

Enoch turned round. His feet dragged themselves slowly across to the table.

He put his hands on the chair. His breath came painfully now. He did not look up.

Auntie May went into the scullery and closed the door behind her. She held onto the edge of the sink and tried not to listen. Something, a feeling, told her that Stephen hit him harder if she stayed.

At last it stopped. Shaking and wretched, Enoch felt Uncle Stephen pick him up in his hard arms. He ran up the stairs with him, flung him down on his bed and banged the door. Enoch sobbed as he crawled under the covers.

Uncle Stephen went back downstairs to the kitchen, and cut himself another piece of cheese.

'So how did the little devil come to break your best china, May?' he asked good-humouredly after a couple of mouthfuls.

'I couldn't take my oath it was him,' Auntie May fretted. 'Only I don't see who else it could have been. I went into the front room this morning to air it and to dust, when I noticed that the cabinet door was ajar. Then the egg man came banging on the back door so I went to see to that. When I came back the cabinet was closed again, but some of the plates at the front near the glass were in pieces.'

'Was this after I'd left for work?'

Auntie May nodded.

'Our two had gone to school. Enoch was upstairs. I went up to the bedroom, and I wasn't inside the door before Enoch called out, "It wasn't me that broke your china, Auntie May!" '

'He did it, no question,' said Uncle Stephen. 'Just trying to shift the blame.'

Auntie May nodded, then nodded again, as if his conviction had revived her own.

'Shall we go and view the body, then?' Uncle Stephen suggested lightly.

The front parlour was a little used place with striped wallpaper and a horsehair sofa. The cold smell of lavender and polish struck them as Uncle Stephen flung open the door.

'Here we are – what the devil?'

From the cabinet came noises of furious destruction, the crash of china and a monstrous howling. Uncle Stephen took a step back, superstitious dread filling his mind with thoughts of demons. Auntie May, thinking only of her precious plates, ran forward. She opened the cabinet and screamed. Shards of Crown Derby flew out over her and with them a bundle of claws and teeth and bristling ginger fur. The animal clung to her, spitting, then leapt down and streaked out of the room.

'Gingerbread!' exclaimed Auntie May. 'I must have shut her in somehow. Perhaps I closed the door when I heard the egg man.'

'For God's sake, May!' Uncle Stephen shouted. 'Of all the stupid things you've done, that's the stupidest I've ever had the misfortune to witness!'

Auntie May bowed her head meekly. She knew her husband well. A nasty scare was the very worst thing for his temper.

'But what about Enoch?' she asked. 'Oh dear, I must run up and see him.'

But Uncle Stephen disagreed.

'It doesn't do, May. Never apologise to children, and never, ever admit a mistake. It only confuses them. You don't want Enoch to lose all confidence in my judgement, do you?'

Slowly Auntie May shook her head.

'Take him up some tea and bread and jam in a while. But get him to apologise before you give it him. And we'll say no more about it after that.'

Grandad had come to Enoch, as he always did. He had carried him to his own room, murmuring comfort. Now Enoch lay face down on the bed while the old man stooped over him, soothing the weals on his bottom with zinc ointment.

'They won't spoil you,' he said grimly as Enoch

winced under his gentle touch. He pulled the covers up round him. 'Mind you lie still, now.'

Slowly he crossed the room to the wardrobe where he kept his medicaments. Then Enoch felt the bed creak and the mattress grow sloping under him as his grandfather eased himself stiffly in at the other side.

'Your Uncle Stephen might have benefited from a few beatings himself,' Grandad said. 'But I could never bear to do it. I can't abide the idea of hitting children. You can't change a boy's nature with the stick.'

Enoch turned his head. 'What about my dad? Did he need beating?'

His grandfather frowned faintly. 'Robert, do you mean? Oh, he was a restless lad. He could never settle to anything. We were always at odds. It's funny how petty all of it seems now that he's gone. He was a handsome fellow, always laughing, with a pretty girl on his arm. He ran through my money, laughing. That was Robert. When I bought him out of the army I swore it was the last help he would get from me. It wasn't, of course.'

Enoch shook his head. 'He was a miner, not a soldier. Daniel told me.'

Grandad smiled. 'That was later. He tried half a dozen professions before he fell to that and married your mother.' He paused, then added, 'Did your mother tell you that we quarrelled about God?'

Enoch nodded.

'I wouldn't fall in with her narrow-minded ideas. it hurt Robert to see us fighting, so I stayed away. After the accident I should have tried to help her. But I was in a terrible state. I had lost my son, and because of Ellen I hadn't seen him for over a year. I told myself that if she suffered hardship she deserved it.'

Enoch lay back and tried to get it straight in his mind. All those hungry years might have been different. But Mam had fought with Grandad. Grandad had hardened his sore heart. That was how things happened. That was how it was.

He was comfortable now, his bottom stinging and radiating a not unpleasant heat. He felt dreamily calm, though he knew the bad pain would come back later. That thought led in a different direction.

'Do you love Uncle Stephen?' he asked suddenly. 'I hate him.'

His grandfather was silent.

'I love him,' he said finally. 'He is my son. You can never stop loving your own child, Enoch. No matter what they do, no matter what happens, you love them.' Enoch's lips formed themselves into a little circle of astonishment.

'Really and truly?'

'Really and truly.' His grandfather looked down at him and smiled.

Enoch lay still, trying to imagine Mam loving him. Instead, Daniel and Polly came into his mind.

'I wish you had known Daniel, Grandad,' he said sleepily. 'And I wish you could be friends with Polly. I don't know what it is about Polly that makes Mam angry. She's always been so good to me.'

His grandfather was silent for a moment. Then he said: 'I know how much Polly loves you, Enoch. She came to the farm yesterday, when you were down in the cow pasture with Edy and your aunt.'

'What!' Enoch tried to sit up, but his grandfather prevented him.

'No, lie still, and I'll tell you. It was lucky I was the only one in the house. Your uncle would have been angry that she came.'

'What did she want?' Enoch asked breathlessly.

'To see you, of course. Someone called Mrs Liverstitch let her know you were here. But I had to tell Polly to stay away, Enoch. I said it was better left. You'd only suffer for it from your uncle if she kept on coming here.'

Enoch felt like crying. 'I wish I'd seen her.'

His grandfather stroked his head gently.

'I told her you were well, and what a clever boy you are getting to be. She wanted to know all about your reading and the chats we have. I told her I would look after you.'

Enoch shut his eyes, imagining Polly standing looking round at the farmyard. He wished he could have shown her his bedroom window, and how high he could go on the swing.

'But she knows I'm here,' he whispered. 'She's seen where I live.'

Relief and happiness flowed through him.

He twisted round to look at his grandfather.

'What is it about Polly that makes everyone drive her away?' he asked. 'Even you did it, Grandad, and you're such a good man.'

His grandfather winced.

'If this was my roof, Polly could stay, and welcome,' he said. 'But it's not. I can't explain to you about Polly now, Enoch. You're too little. But something happened to her that the world can be very cruel about.'

'But Polly's not wicked?' Enoch asked fearfully.

'Certainly not.'

'Promise you'll explain when I'm bigger.'

'I promise.'

Enoch yawned, and stretched himself out. His grandfather saw his tense little body relax.

'You try and sleep now,' he said gently. 'I'll put out the light.'

'I didn't smash those plates, you know,' Enoch said sleepily a moment later.

'Enoch, I will not tolerate a lie!'

'I didn't.' He raised himself on one elbow and met his grandfather's anger with perfect calm. 'All I did was put Gingerbread in the cupboard. She smashed the plates.'

His grandfather made a peculiar noise, a kind of snort while he tried to keep his face straight.

'I believe you,' he said gravely. 'But beware of casuistry, Enoch. It is a Roman Catholic vice, not a Protestant one.'

Enoch let the lovely new word linger in his mind. Tomorrow he would get Grandad to tell him what it meant. Now all he wanted to do was to sleep.

'Well, I shan't do it again,' he murmured as he snuggled down. 'I can be a good boy now Polly knows I'm here. I want to stay with you, Grandad. I don't need them to send me home.'

8

Starting school

'Come along, you great lummock, or we'll be here till nightfall.'

Edy had hold of Enoch's arm, trying to pull him away from the frozen brown puddle he was smashing with the heel of his boot. He shook her arm off, and ran round the other side of the ditch out of reach, then stood staring at her with his alert brown eyes. He would have to go in the end, he knew, but he was determined not to go without a fight.

'Oh, I wish I could be like Harold, and just run ahead and leave you,' she said bitterly. 'Why does Mam always make me do things? I hate being a girl.'

The frost of the February morning had caught Edy's lungs, making her wheeze and cough. She looked longingly down the road that led towards Woodville and school.

'Are you making us late on purpose? You won't like what they'll do to you if you're late.' She held out one hand and brought the other down hard on it to show him. 'Thwack! Thwack! With a leather strap as wide as a man's hand. You won't like that on your first day, will you?'

'I don't want to go,' Enoch said sulkily. 'Harold told me what it's like, and it's horrible. Anyhow, I don't need to go. I can read to Grandad and do my numbers at home, like I did with Daniel.'

'You have to go, Enoch, so shut your gob.'

Edy was getting desperate. Far down the road, the last child ahead of them was disappearing down the dip into Woodville. Putting on a smile, she tried a different tack.

'I've got a toffee in my pocket. If we get to school on time, you can have it. How's that?'

Enoch considered. Edy was treacherous. Her promises were rarely to be trusted. But he was getting restless and uncertain. It was easy enough to defy Edy, but behind her stood the authority of Uncle Stephen, and the might of the teachers with their straps and canes.

'All right,' he said unexpectedly. He danced out of

the ditch and set off at a run, so that Edy had to scamper to catch up.

They hurried down the road, little more than a track, with its glittering hedges and skirt of frozen mud. Through the gaps in the branches they saw the bare flat fields stretching away on either side. The long chimneys and domed ovens of the Woodville potteries came into sight through the haze of frost and smoke. Enoch stopped running, and slowed down again, so that Edy started poking him impatiently in the back. He buried his chin in the folds of his muffler and breathed through the wool until it grew comfortingly warm and wet. School would be all right, he told himself. Grandad said it would be. Only he kept remembering the scary things Harold had whispered to him in bed last night.

Now they were passing the first red brick cottages. Enoch grew more afraid. He could hear hollow screams and shouts coming from down the street. When they came to the gate, he looked up and saw the building, big and black as a chapel, with the hard paved yard in front. Edy pushed him in the gate so hard he fell down and bumped his chin.

'And if you think you're getting a toffee after the dance you led me, you're the biggest fool in England,' she added scornfully, going off to find her friends.

Enoch got up cautiously, putting some spit on his chin to take the sting away. A bell had started to clang, and children started to bang into him as they pushed their way somewhere – he couldn't see exactly where. Then he saw a word written high up on the building, carved into the stone like a dedication. BOYS. 'And the big boys – you just wait and see what they'll do to you,' Harold's whisper was greedily excited in the dark. 'They'll shove your head down the lav and hold you there till they drown you.'

The crowd was pushing behind him, latecomers trying to get ahead. He couldn't wriggle a way through them. His body went stiff and passive, and he allowed himself to be swept in through the door with them all. Inside there were whitewashed walls beaded with damp and rows of wooden pegs. Boys swarmed between the rows of pegs and benches, hanging up their coats and caps. Everybody seemed to know what to do and nobody paid Enoch any heed. He unwound his muffler and hung it over an empty peg, number thirty-six. He took off his cap, but could not bring himself to abandon it. The other boys were pushing through a door at the far side of the cloakroom. Stuffing his cap down the leg of his trousers, Enoch followed them. He stopped just inside the door of the high-ceilinged classroom. More whitewash. A dark mass of desks and benches and a horrible silence. With care, boys slid past him into their places, and sat, arms folded and faces rigid. There were rows and rows of them, all silent. All staring. Enoch stared back and the scared feeling swelled until it was like a big black bag, with him tiny inside. He wanted to curl up with his arms around his head. Instead he stood, holding on to the door.

'New boy?'

Enoch swivelled round.

The speaker was a tall man with black whiskers and a shabby black coat, sitting at a high desk facing the boys.

'New boy?'

The words were repeated impatiently before Enoch was halfway to the desk. He had forgotten about the teacher. He nodded fearfully.

'You must say "Yes, sir". You must always call me "sir" or "Mr Samson".'

Enoch nodded again. The words would not come out, somehow. All the boys in the class were staring at him, and Mr Samson stared too. Their faces were cold and unfriendly, as though they knew something bad about him.

'Name?'

His mouth opened and shut. He was frightened to

say. Mr Samson might have been told things. Mam might have been in to warn him.

'It's Enoch.' He struggled out with it at last. 'Enoch Kirk.'

To his relief Mr Samson's stern expression did not change to anything worse. The teacher ran his finger down a list in a big black book. Then he sent Enoch to an empty place at the end of the bench where the smallest boys were sitting. All the while, there was scarcely a murmur from the forty boys in the big room.

Mr Samson started to call the register. As he barked out names and the boys shouted in response, Enoch folded his arms and sat up straight like the others. Cautiously he let his gaze range around the classroom. Up on the wall there was a map of the world, like the one Grandad had shown him in a book, with the countries of the Empire coloured in red. There was another map done in lots of different colours, with a name he could not read. The other charts had easy words on them in big letters. Behind Mr Samson's desk there was a blackboard like a giant slate with baby sums on it like the sums Daniel used to show him. He'd done much harder work with Grandad recently. He wasn't afraid now, he was beginning to get excited. This was the place Daniel had talked about so much, the place he had hated leaving and had longed to come back to as a teacher. Enoch felt suddenly close to Daniel again and tears pricked at the back of his eyes. He turned his head away, blinking hard. It was then that he saw the books. There was an alcove stuffed full of them, shelves and shelves. There were so many that some had spilled down onto the floor and lay in untidy piles. Enoch stared, and sucked in a huge breath of the stale and chalky air. Grandad was right. This was the place for him.

Girls' voices began to chant in the classroom next door. Enoch, turning his head cautiously, caught a glimpse of Harold two rows behind. Suddenly there was a clatter at the door, and Mr Samson was saying, 'Not a very propitious start, to be late on your first morning. What name?'

Enoch looked up, and looked away quickly, his stomach contracting painfully. He had forgotten about Stephen. He had willed himself to forget. His brother walked down the room and climbed onto the bench beside him. He could feel Stephen's shoulder against his own, Stephen's boot knocking against his underneath the desk. He made himself look again. He saw thick brown hair, dark eyes in a scared white face that was almost his own. But it hurt too much to be near Stephen, knowing that Mam's hands had carefully combed his hair and buttoned up his coat, thinking that perhaps Mam had walked him to the gate and left him with a kiss.

'And Standards Three and Four, slates out please, to complete the sums on the blackboard. Meanwhile, you infants at the front . . .'

Enoch was on his feet. He stared round wildly. He had to do something. He had to get away from Stephen. It hurt too much. Next to Stephen, everyone would see the badness in him, everyone would see what Mam saw.

'Ann is ill!' he shouted.

Mr Samson's pointer wavered and fell.

'I beg your pardon – Kirk, isn't it?'

'Ann is ill, sir. Enoch Kirk, sir. I can read it, Mr Samson.' He pointed to the wall chart.

> 'Ann is ill
> Take a pill
> Do not cry
> A hot pie'

The veterans among the infants, disturbed by this individual outbreak, began to repeat the words in a slow ragged chant, until Mr Samson silenced them with an impatient bellow.

'And I can do sums like that,' Enoch threw in, pointing at the blackboard. 'They're easy.'

Even if it landed him next to Harold, he had to get away.

'Well, well,' Mr Samson seemed more irritated than impressed. 'There's clearly been some muddle made. You should have told me that you'd been to school before.' He turned away to write something in the register, then he called up to Enoch.

'Step into the next row, Kirk. Do you see that empty place? You may sit there for the time being. Standard One.'

Enoch sat down in his new place thankfully. He was still aware of exactly where Stephen was in front of him, but it would not matter. Now nothing would stop him learning, he thought fiercely. Nothing.

That evening at tea Auntie May asked Enoch how he liked school.

'It was lovely,' Enoch said. 'Mr Samson's put me up into Standard One.'

'Standard One already?' his grandfather exclaimed. His voice was very dry to hide his pride. 'We should have sent you to another school. This one will have given you a leaving certificate by the end of the week.'

'What's good enough for my son is good enough for

him,' Uncle Stephen pronounced, banging his cup down on to the table.

'It isn't good enough for either of them,' Grandad retorted. 'If you'd let me use my money to secure their education instead of tying it up in this failure of a farm –'

Auntie May rushed in loudly, 'But you never told me how you got that graze on your chin, Enoch.'

'Fell over,' said Enoch, with a quick glance at Edy, who smirked across at Harold.

'Well I hope you'll be more careful tomorrow,' Auntie May said. 'I don't want to be scraping mud off your clothes every evening.'

After tea, Enoch and his grandfather went into the front parlour.

'What was it really like today?' Grandad asked quietly.

Enoch looked troubled.

'The books are lovely. But I don't like Stephen. Mam should have sent him to another school. Everyone will find out that we don't live in the same house. Everyone will know it's because there's something wrong with me.'

His grandfather took his hand.

'Some people will use it against you,' he said. 'The kind who are always looking for a way to bully and tease. But anyone who takes the trouble to know you, to see what's inside –'

He paused.

'Yes?' Enoch waited fearfully.

'They will be your friends.'

'Mam knows me,' Enoch said in a desolate whisper.

'Does she? Does she really?' His grandfather took him onto his lap. 'Then why doesn't she see the wonders I see in this little package, eh?'

He stroked Enoch's head and held him closer.

'Don't blame Stephen for how you feel,' he added gently. 'He didn't choose to be the one at home. For all you know, he thinks of you with envy.'

Enoch nodded.

'Anyway,' Grandad said. 'I'm glad you don't live with your Mam. Who would I have then?'

9

The first friend

In spite of his talk with Grandad, Enoch hated being in school with Stephen. When he arrived at the school gate, he scanned the yard. If he saw Stephen, he made his way to the opposite corner of the playground. When it was time to go into class he walked past Stephen's desk with his head down. He hated it that Stephen's name came just next to his in the register. Everyone must know they were brothers. Everyone must know which one had been sent away from home.

Stephen seemed to know all the boys from Church Gresley, and played easily with this gang or that. At break-time Enoch walked slowly round the yard by himself or stood by the gate, his hand sliding up and down the iron railings. No one asked him to play. He watched the complicated patterns of chase and tag as the boys whooped up and down the yard, scattering and gathering like birds. Stephen was always there, in the heart of the game, laughing and breathless. Enoch tried to imagine taking a step towards the boys, moving around the edge of the game. But he was too scared of being shouted at, laughed at, pushed away. They had Stephen. Why should they want him?

Then one morning a strange thing happened. Stephen broke away from the game and ran past where Enoch was standing alone at the edge of the yard. He swooped past him again, nearer this time. He circled Enoch once more, and then came to a halt, close enough to touch. Enoch felt something near to panic.

'Why don't you play?'

'What?'

Stephen said it again. 'Why don't you play? Don't you want to?'

Enoch only stared at him. He couldn't speak. It was too much to put into words.

'You can join in, if you want.'

But Enoch only shook his head. After a moment, Stephen gave an awkward sort of nod and ran back to his game.

From that time Enoch felt a strange mixture of repulsion and attraction to his brother. He was scared of seeing Stephen, and yet he didn't want to let him out of his sight. He tried to find out about Stephen's life outside school, where he went and what he did. At first he was able ask Harold, who often went with a gang of boys, including Stephen, on to the common after school. But Harold quickly grew impatient of Enoch's persistent questions. He suspected Enoch of wanting to join his gang, and was determined not to let him.

'If you want to know about Stephen, why don't you talk to him yourself?'

But that was just what Enoch couldn't do.

The only other boy at school Enoch even noticed was the one who sat next to him in class. He was called Matthew Davis, and he was the oldest boy in Standard One, a skinny undersized fellow of nearly ten. He couldn't answer even the simplest question Mr Samson asked him. At first Enoch joined in the laughter rippling round the classroom whenever Matthew got it wrong. Then he saw the way Matthew's head went down in defeat. When Mr Samson scolded him, Matthew's fingers twisted together painfully under the bench. Enoch noticed the great holes in Matthew's boots and his stockings, the baggy jumper and trousers he wore every day regardless of the weather. Outside in the playground Matthew was always at the edge of things. He was clumsy and slow at football, and the other boys rounded on him fiercely if he made a mistake. When the bullying got too much, Matthew retreated, like Enoch, to the edge of the yard.

One dinner-time Matthew was standing quite close by when Enoch got out the food Auntie May had packed for him. As he began on the cold slice of pie, he noticed Matthew's hungry eyes fixed on every mouthful he took.

'What's the matter with you?' Enoch asked irritably. 'Eat your own dinner if you're hungry.'

'I haven't got one today,' Matthew said. 'There wasn't anything in the house this morning.'

Enoch stared. 'What, nothing?'

Matthew shook his head. 'My Granny does washing to keep us, and she hasn't been well. If you can't work, you can't eat, can you?'

Enoch looked inside his bag. He had a brawn sandwich, a couple of apples and a slice of cake, as well as the pie. Auntie May always gave him too much. Silently, he took out the sandwich and one of the apples, and handed them to Matthew.

Matthew's eyes glistened. He didn't speak either. He was too hungry. He tore into the sandwich as if he hadn't seen food for days. He crunched the apple up in great bites. Then he gave a huge burp.

'Thanks. I feel all right now. Sometimes in class, if I've not eaten, I get a bit faint like. I can't properly understand what Samson says, and everybody laughs.'

'You mean you're hungry nearly all the time?'

Matthew nodded.

Enoch shivered a little. He hadn't forgotten how that felt. 'You can have half of my cake too, if you like.'

'Cake!' Matthew turned his share over and over in his hands, looking and smelling, before taking an enormous mouthful.

Enoch, watching him, made up his mind to ask Auntie May for extra tomorrow.

'You don't live with your Mam, then?' he asked Matthew.

It mattered to him very much that Matthew should not.

Matthew shook his head.

'Dead,' he said indistinctly. 'And my Dad. There's just me and Granny now.' He grinned. 'Granny says, "Just you and me, lad, against the world!"'

Very much to his surprise, Enoch realised he liked Matthew. He had made his first friend.

After that, Matthew and Enoch spent their time in the playground together. Enoch still needed to track

Stephen, and Matthew accepted this as part of Enoch, along with his cleverness and his glorious farm provisions.

'I just wish I could see what he does outside school,' Enoch exclaimed in frustration, as he and Matthew piled out of the school gates at the end of the day. 'Auntie May won't let me go out of the farm after tea. She says I'm too young.'

'Well, I could tell you,' Matthew said. 'Granny lets me go out as I like, once I've finished my jobs at home. They mostly go to the common, don't they? I've seen them there.'

'You can be my spy!' Enoch exclaimed in delight. 'We'll have our own gang, Matthew, a spying gang. Harold thinks he's so great to have a gang, but I've got one too now.'

So Matthew trailed after Harold and Stephen as they roamed over the fields and the common, catching and cooking rabbits, robbing birds' nests and fishing in the stream.

Sometimes Harold caught him, and it took the best part of Enoch's lunch to persuade him that black eyes and bruises were part of the business of being a spy.

'You don't seem to land many, though,' Matthew said looking at him plaintively while chewing bread and cheese.

'That's because I'm the leader,' Enoch explained. 'Harold's their leader, and I'm ours. I have to think the things up, and you do 'em. Now, let's get your arithmetic book out, and I'll explain to you what Samson was doing on the board this morning.'

Matthew smiled. He didn't mind the lessons part of the gang nearly so much. Things that seemed impossibly complicated when Mr Samson said them turned out to be quite simple when Enoch went over them with him. Matthew had given the right answer in class three times in a week, and Mr Samson's face started to wear a look of hope when he put his hand up.

'Enoch's made a friend,' said Harold in his sneering way at tea one evening. 'That booby Matthew Davis. Best he could manage, I suppose.'

'Is he a nice boy, Enoch?' Auntie May said, frowning at Harold.

Enoch nodded. 'He's teaching me how to whistle, and I'm teaching him how to read.'

Auntie May looked taken aback.

'He's can't read yet? Is he a very little boy?'

'Just a hungry one,' said Enoch.

'His granny's a washerwoman,' guffawed Harold. 'Matthew has to help her wash other people's bloomers.'

'Bring him home with you after school, Enoch,' Grandad said in his kind way. 'I'd be interested to meet him.'

'A washerwoman's grandson,' murmured Auntie May. 'I'm no prouder than the next person, but do you really think . . .?'

Enoch and his grandfather met each other's eyes.

'I'm glad he's your friend,' said Grandad.

10

The surprise

Enoch was going into the kitchen for a drink of water one evening when he caught part of a conversation between Auntie May and Uncle Stephen.

'The others all have them,' said Auntie May with unusual force. 'And I don't see why Enoch shouldn't. He's settled down nicely, and he helps to me round the place, which is more than Harold does. It isn't right just to ignore it. While he's with us, we should treat him near enough like we treat our own.'

Enoch retreated rapidly. He didn't want to hear what Uncle Stephen had to say about him. It was enough to catch Uncle Stephen's glare if he dared to help himself to seconds at the dinner table. He wondered if he should ask Grandad about what he had heard, but decided against it. Very soon he forgot all about it himself.

It was late March and the daffodils were out. Every green thing was shooting up outside, and Enoch wondered confusedly if that was why Auntie May kept measuring him. She made him stretch out his arms while she held the tape measure this way and that. Then she stood, lips pursed, eyeing him up and down. Auntie May was acting strangely, and it wasn't only measuring. When he ran home from school ahead of the others, bursting into the kitchen with a cheery shout, Auntie May looked flustered, and bundled things quickly up off the kitchen table into a corner. He turned to Grandad for an explanation, but he only smiled and shook his head.

Edy seemed to be in on the secret, whatever it was. In the evenings, when Enoch looked up from his book, he would find Edy watching him, a knowing smile on her face. But the strangest thing was when Harold rather glumly took a knife to his china piggy bank one Saturday morning.

'What are you going to buy?' Enoch asked enviously. Apart from the odd penny from Grandad or Auntie May, he got no pocket money. Uncle Stephen was quite strict about that.

'Something Mum's making me get. You'll find out.'

He looked at Enoch oddly. 'You really have no idea, have you?'

'Idea of what?'

But Harold ran whistling down the stairs and was gone.

The following Monday Enoch woke to find that Harold was out of bed before him. As he sat up, he heard his grandfather's slow tread on the landing, and Edy calling down excitedly to her mother in the kitchen. Alarmed, Enoch jumped out of bed. Why had they let him oversleep? Quickly he pulled on his trousers and jumper, and made for the door.

'He's coming down, Mam!' Harold shouted from the bottom of the stairs.

Enoch stood at the door, too scared to move. What sort of trick were they playing? He didn't want to go down and find out. But surely Grandad wouldn't let anything bad happen to him? Surely Auntie May wouldn't turn on him? He forced himself to walk out and down the stairs.

When Enoch came into the room the family were all standing round the table, waiting for him. Then they all started to sing, even Uncle Stephen, and Enoch saw the pile of presents by his plate, and understood.

'Happy birthday, Enoch!' Auntie May scooped him up and gave him a kiss.

'Did you really not guess?' Edy demanded suspiciously.

Enoch shook his head. He did not trust himself to speak. He sat down at the table and, picking up the topmost present, turned it over and over in his hands.

'Aren't you going to open them, then?' Harold called impatiently.

He watched, sharp-eyed, as Enoch unwrapped each present. From his grandfather there was a big new storybook and some soldiers as good as Harold's. Auntie May had made him a set of new shirts, and Edy gave him some handkerchiefs she'd embroidered with his initial. Harold had bought him a tin whistle.

Enoch looked round at them all, his eyes shining.

'Thank you,' he said. 'Thank you. It's –' he shrugged, speechless.

'You got more off Grandad than I did,' Harold muttered.

'Harold!' his mother shushed him.

'I – hem, I haven't a sixpence for you today, but you will have it at the beginning of next month,' Uncle Stephen promised Enoch in a unique burst of generosity.

'If you want to bring someone home for your birthday tea, you're more than welcome,' said Auntie May with a warm smile. Her smile vanished as she said hastily, 'Perhaps not that boy Matthew, though.'

'What about your brother, Enoch?' Grandad asked in his deep voice. 'Would you like Stephen to come?'

'Your Mam too, if you like,' added Auntie May.

Enoch's hand crept along the table to take his Grandad's.

'But I live here now,' he said. 'I don't want Mam coming. Or Stephen.'

'I'd like Stephen to come,' said Harold. 'But Enoch hates him, don't you, Enoch? He won't even speak to him at school.'

'Is that so, Enoch?' his grandfather asked him with a look of gentle concern. 'Do you still not play with your brother?'

Enoch shook his head.

'I've got a friend,' he said stubbornly, 'and that's Matthew. I'm much too busy playing with him.'

Enoch took his whistle and one of his handkerchiefs to school to show Matthew. He felt bad when he saw how Matthew's face looked.

'I'll lend you the whistle when it's not so new,' he promised. 'And I'll bring you some of the cake tomorrow. I wish you could come back and have some today, but Auntie May said not.'

'I've never had presents on my birthday,' said

Matthew. 'The most Granny can manage is sugar buns at tea-time.'

'I never had presents before,' Enoch said defensively. 'Not when I was living at Mam's.'

'Really? But your Mam gave Stephen some marbles for his birthday. I saw him show them to Harold, remember?'

Enoch stuffed his presents abruptly back in his pockets.

'I'm bored talking about birthdays,' he said. 'I won't let you share my dinner if you keep on, Matthew.'

But at teatime, when they sang for him again and Auntie May brought in a cake with six bright candles, Enoch felt nothing but happiness. He didn't want it ever to end, this birthday feeling. He didn't want to have to blow the candles out.

'Did you make a wish?' Auntie May asked.

Enoch nodded.

'Tell us, then,' said Edy.

'Don't be a tease,' said Auntie May. 'You know if you tell it, it doesn't come true.'

'This one can't come true anyway,' Enoch said. 'It won't matter if I tell. I was just wishing Polly could have seen my cake, that's all.'

'Polly?' said Auntie May uneasily. 'Now what made you think of Polly all of a sudden?'

'I miss her,' Enoch said simply. 'I haven't seen her since I came here. I want to tell her all about school and I want her to see my presents.'

Uncle Stephen glared at Auntie May.

'Don't nod your head at him so sympathetically. You know I will not have that young woman under my roof. She's no better than she should be.'

'That's not the sort of language I expect to hear at this table,' Grandad said sharply.

'What does it mean?' Enoch asked.

But Grandad, usually so quick to explain new words, said nothing.

'Can I have some more cake?' Harold cut in impatiently. 'That's the second time I've asked, but you're all too busy talking to listen to me.'

Auntie May cut Harold an extra large slice and began to talk brightly about the weather.

After tea, Enoch retreated to the front parlour with Grandad.

'Now will you explain what Uncle Stephen said about Polly?' he demanded.

Grandad shook his head.

'There's no need to explain ill manners and ignorance,' he said curtly. 'But I am glad you thought of Polly today, Enoch, because she thought of you.'

Enoch's heart began to beat very fast.

'What do you mean?'

'This packet was left on the doorstep, addressed to me.' Grandad pulled a small brown parcel out of his coat pocket. 'I told your aunt it might be a religious pamphlet I was expecting.'

'But it's really from Polly?'

Enoch reached out with eager, timid fingers. His grandfather had cut the string, but the contents were still inside. Enoch pulled out a little sugar mouse, and a note. He put the note down carefully and balanced the mouse on the palm of his hand. It was pink and heavy, with two black dots for eyes and a thread of a tail. He smelt its faint vanilla scent, and reached out with just the tip of his tongue to taste its sweetness.

Suddenly he realised.

'It's to remind me of the other one,' he said. 'My toy mouse was a birthday present after all.'

The knowledge filled him with happiness. He had been too little to know, but Polly had remembered his birthday, even at Mam's.

He reached into his shirt. Discoloured and shabby, the cloth mouse was introduced to the sugar mouse.

'They'll live together,' Enoch announced. 'My mice from Polly.'

'Not in your shirt, though,' said Grandad hastily.

'I've got an old money-box you can have, with a little key. That'll keep them safe. Don't you want to read her note now?'

Enoch held it for a moment before he looked. The words were written in a simple clear hand. 'Thinking of you today as always. All my love, Polly.'

'She won't ever forget me,' Enoch whispered. 'That's what it means, isn't it, Grandad?'

The old man nodded.

'I wish I could write back. I can write so well now. I could tell her all about school and my birthday, and my friend Matthew. Don't you know where she's living, Grandad? Don't you have her address?'

He shook his head.

'She didn't put it on the note. Your Mam would know, but I doubt she'd tell me. Your aunt could find out, but she wouldn't want you writing. Best leave it, Enoch. I know how hard it is.'

Enoch's mouth trembled. He rubbed his hand over his eyes.

'I'll never forget her,' he said fiercely. 'No matter how much they want me to.'

11

Fight!

Next morning Enoch's birthday was all but forgotten by the family. Auntie May broke a cream jug and Uncle Stephen shouted. Harold was already regretting the truce of the day before, and boxed Enoch's ears twice before breakfast. On the way to school it was raining, hard slanted spring rain, and all the classroom windows were shut against it. The smell of wet boots mingled with the smells of ink and dust and stale woolen clothes. By late morning the air was heavy and warm, and some of the infants, nearest the coal stove, were barely awake.

Enoch, who had filled his slate with sums, bent over his desk as though he was still busy. He was thinking about yesterday. His birthday had been something wonderful, like a treasure he could keep and hold, turning it over and over in his hands. Grandad had given him the money-box for all the things he had from Polly. The key was on a bit of string around his neck. He could feel it there now, safe under his clothes. His birthday made him glad to be at the farm. Auntie May and Grandad loved him, and even the others liked him a bit. He felt settled now. Perhaps tonight when he was alone with Grandad he could talk some more about Stephen and the strange scared feelings he still had about Mam at home.

Matthew sighed suddenly, bringing Enoch's mind back to the present. Then someone dropped their slate with a clatter that brought Mr Samson's head sharply up.

He let out an impatient exclamation.

'Simmonds, ring the bell for the end of morning school. Davis, collect up Standard Three's books. Standard Two, leave your slates on your desks. I will correct your work first thing this afternoon.'

With a clatter of boots, but no talking, the boys made their way down the classroom and out into the cloakroom. As soon as Mr Samson was out of sight there was an explosion of noise. Boys pushed and pulled each other, shouted, hopped, and banged on the benches in sheer relief. Enoch wandered over to the window, and began to draw on it idly with his finger. He felt someone come up behind him. It was Matthew.

'I was wondering if you was getting your dinner out,' he said hopefully. 'Granny gave me some too today. I thought we could share.'

'No, wait a minute,' said Enoch. He had seen something outside. Harold and Stephen, pulling on their coats, had just dashed across the rain-swept yard towards the gate. Enoch turned and pushed past Matthew.

'Where are you going?' Matthew called after him. 'Is it something for the gang?'

Enoch shouted back something incomprehensible and made for the door.

'But it's pouring down!' Matthew exclaimed. He stood for a moment, irresolute, then ran after his friend.

Enoch was outside, in the empty yard. The rain tumbled down on him as he stood, fists clenched, watching the wind rippling across the long brown puddles.

'I've lost them,' Enoch said. 'They're not here.'

'They'll have to come back for afternoon school, or Mr Samson'll whop'em,' said Matthew practically.

'But what are they doing now?' Enoch's cry was despairing.

'Having a pee is the most likely,' said Matthew. 'Or did one of them forget his dinner? Don't be daft, Enoch. Let's get inside before we're soaked through.'

He put his hand on Enoch's shoulder and began to pull him towards the door. Reluctantly, Enoch allowed himself to move. Then, just as they reached the doorway, Harold and Stephen came out from round the corner of the building. They stood side by side, blocking the door.

'I told you,' said Harold triumphantly, 'I told you he'd come after us, Stephen, him and his pet monkey. He's just a stupid copycat, your brother. Whatever we do, he has to copy. Wherever we go, he's got to follow. Isn't he a case?'

'Shut your great gob, Harold, and let us through,' Matthew told him.

He was big enough to push past Harold into school. 'Come on inside,' he called to Enoch, 'or you won't get your dinner eaten before Samson comes back.'

Enoch tried to catch him up by sliding between the two boys on the step, but Harold reached out and grabbed him.

'I'm fed up with you,' he said fiercely. 'Sixpence of my own money I had to spend on you, and then you play the stupid whistle right in my ear in bed!' He turned to Stephen. 'I'll hold him and you belt him, all right?'

'You just dare!' Matthew shouted. 'It's two against two, fair fight or nothing!'

Stephen looked uncomfortable.

'Let's all just get inside. I hate this bullying stuff of yours, Harold. What's it matter if he follows us about?'

Harold gave Enoch a shove towards Stephen.

'All right,' he snarled. 'If you're so fond of him, you have him. I wish it was you that had to live with him, and not me, that's all!'

He pushed his way past Matthew into school without a backward glance.

Stephen hesitated. He still had hold of Enoch.

'Get off me!' Enoch said roughly.

Stephen let him go and followed him inside.

'Go away a minute, Matthew,' Stephen said. 'I just want to talk to Enoch, all right?'

Matthew looked at Enoch, who nodded. Stephen's face was friendly, and Enoch felt the scared feeling fade a little. Why did he feel so strange about his brother? He didn't want to be with Mam himself any more. He didn't miss that cold hungry house. But Stephen slept in the bed he once shared with Daniel. Stephen walked home past the corner where Polly used to wait. And Stephen had the pleasure of being the good one, the one Mam wanted and loved.

Stephen smiled now and said:

'It was your birthday, wasn't it? Harold said you got presents, and a cake. Auntie May must be a nice person to live with.'

'She is,' Enoch said. He had never got past his fears enough to think whether Stephen was having a nice time with Mam.

'How is it at home?' he asked in a voice that sounded strange to him.

Stephen looked startled.

'It's quiet,' he said at last. 'Compared to where I was, it's quiet.'

They eyed each other for a moment, then Stephen said:

'Well, happy birthday, then. Mam remembered. She said something funny about it.'

Enoch fiddled with the buttons on his coat. He didn't want to know, but he had to.

'What did she say?' he asked reluctantly.

Stephen hesitated. He looked puzzled.

'I didn't really understand the words,' he said. 'Something about it being no cause for celebration.'

To Stephen's complete astonishment, Enoch hit him hard across the ear.

'Enoch, for pity's sake –!'

But he was at it again, banging him on the nose. As a thin trickle of blood ran down onto Stephen's lip, Enoch felt a warm and savage glow.

'Come on, stop it!'

Enoch's answer was a kick.

Then Stephen began to fight back. He hit out and landed a good one on Enoch's check. The big dull pain spread out across Enoch's face. He felt, rather than saw the crowd that rapidly formed round them, raising the chant of 'Fight! Fight! Fight!' that brought more boys running. And there was no doubt who was the better fighter. Enoch could get no more blows in as Stephen grabbed his hair and aimed another kick at his ribs. One more thump, and Enoch was down, sprawling on the wet floor. He covered his head, and waited for Stephen to kick again.

'What – on earth is the matter with you?' Stephen panted.

Then the crowd melted away. The cloakroom was suddenly empty of all but Enoch and Stephen and, in the doorway, his waterproof cape glistening with rain, the terrible figure of Mr Samson.

Joseph Kirk was reading the Bible in bed by candlelight.

113

'What does it say?'

The voice was Enoch's. He was standing by the door in his nightshirt.

'Come and read it for yourself,' the old man said.

Enoch came forward and took the candle, leaning over his grandfather's shoulder. The flame lit up a few inches of small print.

'*Lord, how are they increased that trouble me! Many are they that rise up against me.*

'*Many there be which say of my soul, There is no help for him in God.*'

As Enoch read, his voice trembled, and he had to clench his teeth together to stop himself crying.

'You were in bad trouble today, weren't you?' the old man said gently. Enoch nodded.

'You mustn't be angry with your brother,' his grandfather said. 'I told you before, he didn't choose to be at home. And you are better off here, Enoch. Your mother's house is a poor one.'

'I know it is. But she wants Stephen there and she doesn't want me, and no one will tell me why. That's the trouble. That's still the trouble.'

His grandfather sighed and turned down the bed-clothes.

'Get in.'

Enoch hopped into the warm bed. Curled against

the old man's bony side he began to feel sleepy and comforted.

'Your mother's life has not been an easy one,' the old man said quietly after a while. 'They say that suffering softens people, Enoch, but I have more often seen it turn people to stone. We cannot force people to love us, even if they ought to. But you must know,' he turned to the little boy and smiled, 'you must surely know that you are loved.'

'By you and Polly?'

He nodded.

'By God?'

'Of course.'

Enoch frowned.

'Mam knows more about God than I do.'

His grandfather smiled.

'One can be very certain about things, and yet still be wrong. God may surprise your mother, Enoch. He's bigger than her idea of Him, that's certain.'

'I want to know –' Enoch said breathlessly.

'Know what?'

'Everything. Everything about God, so I know more than Mam does. So I can prove she's wrong when she tries to scare me.'

His grandfather laughed.

'You want to be a theologian now, do you? Well,

I've no doubt you have the brains for it. And I seem to detect a thirst for godliness underlying your criminal exploits.'

Enoch smiled and closed his eyes, understanding the old man's affectionate tone more than his words.

His grandfather blew out the candle, and settled down under the covers.

'I should have done more while I had the chance,' he said, so softly Enoch could barely hear him. 'I could have saved Daniel. I must save this one. There's little enough of my money left now. Still, perhaps something can be done. Perhaps. I must make some plans.'

PART THREE

'She hates me!'

PART THREE

'She hates me!'

12

The funeral party

On the morning of the funeral, Enoch, lying awake, heard Nellie go into the front room and light the fire. He knew Auntie May would be up early too, counting out her silver teaspoons and fetching down the best plates with her own hands. The kitchen door banged, and Enoch guessed it was Uncle Stephen going out to see the cowman. Uncle Stephen was not in the best of tempers. He was only going to the funeral, he said, because Auntie May lacked the courage of her convictions.

'Dig a hole at the bottom of a field and get it over,' he had grumbled at teatime the previous evening. 'Forget all the cant and hocus-pocus. I'm paying a small fortune to feed a lot of people I don't even like, and paying lip service to a ritual that benefits no one except Mr Dawson.'

'You have to respect your father's wishes,' murmured Auntie May.

'Why should I, when he didn't respect mine? It would serve him right if we used him to manure the potatoes.'

He swallowed down his tea and banged out of the door.

Auntie May was too shocked to speak for a moment. Then said to the children in a lowered voice, 'Pay no attention. He's rather upset, I'm afraid. He's had some disappointing news.'

'About money?' said Harold sharply.

Auntie May nodded.

'Your grandfather has done something rather extra-ordinary in his will,' she said in a slightly choked voice. 'But we won't talk about it now.'

Enoch didn't care what excuse she made. He pushed his knife into his bread roll and gave it a vicious twist. He was pretending it was Uncle Stephen.

'Nine year olds don't mess up their bread like that,' said Auntie May with unusual severity. 'I'm surprised at you, Enoch.'

Enoch picked up his roll. Slowly he tore it into pieces and scattered it over the table.

Then he burst into tears and ran up to his room. Auntie May came up a little later, and knocked on the door. When she came into the room he pretended to be asleep. He lay there without moving until the room was dark and Harold came up to bed.

Lying in bed next morning, Enoch could see his new black trousers and coat neatly folded over the back of a chair. He didn't want to put them on. The summer sunshine was leaking round the edges of the curtains and the noises of all living things seemed to be outside. In the bed next to him Harold lay still asleep, the covers bunched up around his shoulders. Carefully Enoch slid out of bed and crept towards the door. He went across the landing and into his grandfather's room. It seemed emptier now that the bed had been stripped, and the mattress lay bare on the high black bedstead. The window was open, and the warm summer sounds outside made the silence stronger. Enoch went over and touched the bed very gently. Grandad had had a stroke a year before his death, which confined him to bed. Enoch had spent his free time sitting by his bed, reading to him, and when he could no longer understand, gently stroking his hand. His grandfather had slipped quietly into death like a child falling asleep after a long day's play. Enoch wanted him so badly. It hurt him like a bruise inside.

Uncle Stephen tied his black tie with the aid of the mirror over the fire in the front room. The table was starting to look presentable, Harold and Edy looked smart in their mourning clothes, and Uncle Stephen felt some cheerfulness returning. He planned to snub Mr Dawson thoroughly by not inviting him back to the house.

'Time to go,' he announced. 'Where's Enoch?'

But Enoch could not be found and Uncle Stephen and his children went off to church without him.

Auntie May, who was staying behind to see to the food, came upon Enoch at last when she went out to feed the hens. He was sitting in the barn doorway, still in his pyjamas, with his arm round the neck of one of the farm dogs. Auntie May strode towards him wrathfully, but a glance at his face silenced her.

'You miss him, don't you?' she said, surprise and guilt in her voice.

Enoch nodded.

None of the others missed Grandad, he knew. Even Auntie May had seemed relieved when the end had come, and the burden of washing and caring for Grandad was lifted.

'Is that why you didn't want to go to church?'

He nodded again, wiping his eyes.

Auntie May took him by the hand and led him into

the house. She helped him get washed and dressed, and found him jobs to do to help her, so that the return of the mourners took them both by surprise.

About twenty people had come back to the house. The men in their Sunday clothes gathered with their backs to the fire, while the women found themselves seats along the chilly edges of the front room. Enoch stood near Auntie May at the table. If he had been younger, he would have held on to her dress. Uncle Stephen busied himself with bottles of beer and sherry at the sideboard. After his second bottle of beer his voice grew louder. Every time he heard Uncle Stephen's booming laugh, Enoch thought of a new way to kill him dead.

'Sherry, Ellen Kirk?'

It caught Enoch painfully in his ribs. He had not dreamt of seeing Mam here, knowing how she felt about Grandad. He went towards the fireplace, as if seeking a place among the men, and got a glimpse of her in the mirror above it. He was afraid to look at her directly. He hadn't been in the same room as her for nearly five years. He watched how her mouth turned down as she waved away the glass Uncle Stephen offered.

Her clothes were the shabbiest in the room. He felt hot inside when he thought how much nicer Auntie

May looked, not old and skinny as a stick. And Stephen, whose hand Mam held, was dressed in his school clothes, with only a black armband for mourning.

Then a tremendous hope took hold of Enoch. He looked wildly round the room. He couldn't see her, but there were people in the way. She might be here. After all, she had no way to let him know. He hadn't heard from Polly in over a year. Auntie had opened all Grandad's letters after he had his stroke. If any came from Polly, she never said. He made his way slowly through the crowded room, looking and looking. Would Uncle Stephen have let her come? He couldn't see Polly anywhere, but Mam was here, and in desperation, Enoch went up to her.

'Is Polly here?'

His mother stared at him, her mouth pouched and sour with disapproval.

'That's a fine greeting, I must say, after all this time. You don't change, do you, Enoch? No, Polly isn't here. Polly left. Didn't you know?'

'Left?' Enoch couldn't take it in. 'Left where? Left Burton? Where did she go?'

His mother's face tightened. 'I don't know where she went. She left with a man, I'm told. I've no idea where she is now.'

'When? When was this?' Enoch demanded urgently.

She looked indifferent. She couldn't even remember exactly. 'A while back. Maybe a year ago.'

'No.' Enoch shook his head. 'No, that's impossible. She wouldn't have done that. She wouldn't have gone without saying goodbye.'

His mother dismissed this, sawing the air with an impatient hand. 'Forget about Polly. You can be sure that wherever she is, she's not thinking about any of us.'

Enoch walked slowly away from her. He felt numb, stunned. The pain was small now, dulled by the noise and movement all around him, but he was frightened of what would happen when the people went away. He hadn't seen Polly for so long, but it felt like another bereavement to know she had left. There was no one for him now.

The guests were leaving. As his mother got up to go, Enoch saw Uncle Stephen block her path.

'We need to talk,' he said rather beerily.

Ellen Kirk drew back her head and frowned. 'I need to find my boy.'

'There's one of 'em here,' said Uncle Stephen, indicating Enoch. 'You have two you're responsible for, I believe. As far as I'm concerned, you can leave with two.'

'Stephen, please!' Auntie May came in, wiping her

hands on her apron. 'Don't start on that now. Not on the day of the funeral.'

She put her arm round Enoch, and pushed him towards the door.

Uncle Stephen's face took on a belligerent look.

'Let him be, May. Let him listen.'

Unhappily, Aunt May released Enoch. He stayed near the door, and watched Uncle Stephen with open hatred.

'I'm just telling your mother,' Uncle Stephen began, 'I'm just telling her that as far as I'm concerned, we've fed and clothed and paid for you long enough. We're not a charity for those of doubtful breeding. Charity begins at home, and that's where you should be. At home. Not here.'

Ellen Kirk narrowed her eyes.

'You're drunk,' she said with withering scorn. She swept past him to the door.

'Stephen!' she called up the stairs. 'We're off. Now!'

She turned back to Auntie May.

'Get his things packed,' she said. 'I won't take him now, but I'll have him back as soon as you like. I knew he'd not be wanted now.'

Enoch looked over at Auntie May expectantly. She would deny that straight away. Surely she would say she wanted him? But Auntie May wouldn't meet his eye. She looked away across the room and her face turned very red. Enoch began to be afraid.

'Mind you don't forget to send for him,' called Uncle Stephen as his parting shot to Ellen. 'I wouldn't put it past you.'

As she left, Ellen Kirk's glance fell on Enoch's stricken face.

'Well, you needn't look like that,' she said with sudden fury. 'Children are supposed to be glad when they know they're going home!'

Uncle Stephen and Enoch were left alone in the front room together while Auntie May showed the others to the door. Enoch stood pressing his eyes with his fingers, but the tears came anyway. He couldn't seem to stop them. If Uncle Stephen even noticed, he didn't say anything. He wandered over to where the empty bottles stood and shook one after the other fruitlessly.

'He shouldn't have done it,' he said over his shoulder. 'I don't normally get like this. It's just that I'm upset.' He turned round and to Enoch's confusion his face crumpled into grief. 'I needed that money for the farm,' he said. 'He knew I was expecting it.'

Auntie May came bustling back in. She looked at her husband and her voice became very bright and loud.

'Come along, then, Enoch,' she said. 'It's time to get you all packed, isn't it?'

She took his hand, and feeling his wet fingers, looked down at his face in surprise.

'Oh no, Enoch. Don't cry!' She held her apron to his face. 'I can't bear it if you cry.'

Hidden in her apron, in her arms, Enoch began to sob.

'Come now,' said Auntie May. 'Don't you remember, when you first came here, all you wanted was to go home? No one meant you to live with us for ever. It'll be like an adventure, going back again.'

Uncle Stephen walked unsteadily to the door.

'Crybaby,' he mumbled.

To Enoch's astonishment, Auntie May lifted her head and snapped: 'If you're as tipsy as that, Stephen, you might as well put yourself to bed!'

She turned back to Enoch.

'There's nothing wrong with crying,' she said. 'Look,' she showed him her teary fingers. 'I'm doing it too.'

13

Back home to Mam

The next day Enoch set off for Church Gresley, pushing the little handcart that held his things. Auntie May had found him an old tin trunk to put them in. They said goodbye at the door of the farmhouse, Auntie May crying a little and pressing a shilling into his hand.

'I took it out of the egg money,' she whispered. 'Don't tell your uncle.'

Uncle Stephen had been out since early morning. Enoch was glad not to have seen him.

'He told me to say goodbye and good luck,' said Auntie May unconvincingly. 'You'll be back to see us, though, won't you, Enoch?'

Enoch nodded uncertainly. He couldn't imagine

leaving the farm, but coming back to visit seemed even stranger.

To his surprise, Edy had a hug for him and a present, a watch case embroidered with his initials.

'It's lovely, Edy,' he said. 'I'll keep it for when I have a watch.'

Edy turned pink and hot.

'Actually, I made it for Edward Kingham,' she said in a rush. 'Only I don't like him any more, so you can have it.'

That made Enoch laugh, and then, strangely, it made him want to cry, so he turned quickly and set off.

Auntie May had asked Harold to go with Enoch to keep him company, but Harold said he had hurt his foot on the barn swing. It was a relief to Enoch. All morning Harold had been wearing the grin of a boy who was getting his room back. The sheer joy of it had made him nice to Enoch, but Enoch was still glad Harold was staying behind. He needed to make the journey on his own.

The road was dusty and hot in the summer sun, and he often had to stop to rest. The cart was awkward to push, with rough wooden handles that took the skin off his hands. He tried dragging it sometimes. When he reached Church Gresley, he stopped and leant against the cart, just looking. The sky was a hazy blue, and the sunlight made the red brick terraces look almost beautiful. Further up the street he could just see the spire of Mr Dawson's church. There were some small children playing, and a man walking past them with his dog. Nobody noticed Enoch. Leaning there on the cart, he tried to imagine what it would be like. How would he manage to live in his mother's house? He was frightened of losing himself. There would be no one to love him and teach him. There would be no one who believed in him. He was leaving hope behind, walking into the cold and the dark. For a wild moment he thought of running away to London, like in a story. But this little triangle of villages was all he knew. He was too small, too scared. Slowly he straightened himself up and began to pull the handcart towards his mother's house.

He opened the scullery door, and went inside. The kitchen was dark and small and insufferably hot. Stephen was sitting in his shirtsleeves at the table, and his mother was at the range, stirring a saucepan.

'It's me,' Enoch said, though he wanted to say nothing at all. He stood in the doorway, not wanting to step in.

His mother turned round only briefly. She did not smile, nor did he.

'Well, shut the door and come in, then,' she said.

Enoch did as he was told. He was back, then. He was back for good. He felt his mouth tremble, but he was not going to cry. How strange that when he first went to the farm he had wanted this so badly! But he had imagined a welcome, a glad face. That was what Stephen had got. It would be hard to see Mam smile at Stephen. Perhaps that, after all, would be the hardest thing.

Stephen was still staring down at the table. His face wore a closed expression, shy or resentful, Enoch could not tell. Since that fight years ago, Stephen had given up trying to make friends. At school Enoch ignored him. But how could they ignore each other in this tiny house?

'I left my stuff outside,' Enoch said. 'I suppose I shall have to bring it in.'

'Stephen will help you get it upstairs,' his mother replied. Stephen rose slowly to his feet.

'You're in the back bedroom again,' his mother added. 'Where you were with Daniel.'

It was the strangest thing to hear Mam say his name. Enoch waited a moment, but as Mam didn't say any more, he followed Stephen upstairs.

Even on this warm day, the bedroom felt chilly. The faded paper, whitish brown with tiny blue flowers, was stained in places with damp. The tiny grate was covered with dust. Enoch dumped the tin trunk on the floor and stood still, staring round. He did not remember the washstand and the chest of drawers behind the door. Perhaps they had come after Daniel died. He went over to the bed and touched it. It had seemed much higher, much bigger when he lived here before. 'You can have the side next to the window,' Stephen said. 'I sleep this side.' He patted the bed near the wall.

'That used to be my side,' Enoch said. 'Daniel always slept next to the window.'

Enoch bent to look under the bed. He knew there was nothing there, but he wanted to remember.

'When Daniel was alive, he kept his trumpet under here,' he told Stephen. 'And his special box.'

Stephen was faintly embarrassed.

'I wouldn't know about that. The only thing under there now is the pot.'

Slowly Enoch opened the lid of his trunk and began to take out his belongings. 'You've got a lot of clothes,' Stephen said, staring in surprise. He gestured towards the chest of drawers. 'You can put them in there. All but the top drawer. That's mine.'

He sat down on the bed, watching Enoch unpack. Once or twice he leant forward, but Enoch was careful to keep everything out of his reach.

'Didn't Harold have a monkey like that?' Stephen asked, as Enoch set the clockwork toy on the window-sill next to his books. 'He brought it to show me once.'

'Grandad bought us both one,' said Enoch. 'He bought me these soldiers too.' Stephen's eyes widened.

'Lucky you. Will you let me play with them?'

'Course not.'

When everything else was unpacked, Enoch took something out of his pocket and put it under the pillow on his side of the bed.

'What's in that little box?' asked Stephen curiously. 'Something valuable?'

'Mind your own business,' said Enoch.

If Stephen was offended, he didn't show it. He rolled off the bed and onto his feet.

'If you've finished we'd better go down,' he said. 'Mam's cooked something special. I told her she'd better, just to let you down gently like. I know from all Harold's talk how high they like to live up at the farm.'

Enoch felt tears prick behind his eyes. Stephen's kindness got under his defences, however much he wanted to ignore it.

'Thanks,' he said gruffly out loud. 'I am very hungry.'

'Me too.' Stephen gave a tentative smile. 'So we've got that in common, at any rate!'

Downstairs, their mother had cleared the table and set it for tea. When she saw them, she began to dole out something on to plates from a pot on the range. It smelt like stew, and the familiar savoury smell gave Enoch hope. The farm and this house were not such worlds apart. They sat down at the table, Stephen and his mother side by side, with Enoch opposite them. He picked up his knife and fork and speared a piece of potato, only to realise that the other two had bowed their heads. In the silence he awkwardly laid down his cutlery, and then Stephen began to say the blessing. When he finished, Enoch picked up his fork again and began to eat. But the stew was horrible. Mixed in with potato and onion were lumps of fatty mutton that resisted all his efforts at chewing, and when he swallowed them unchewed, he felt as if he was going to be sick. He picked out the bits of potato and onion on his plate and ate them hungrily. Then he put down his knife and fork and pushed away his plate.

His mother looked up.

'You haven't eaten your meat. What's the matter, don't you like it?'

Enoch shook his head.

His mother put down her knife and fork. Her look cowed him. It was the look he remembered. Her disapproval was entire. If she could, she would have rubbed him out like a misspelt word.

'I got that specially for you,' she said slowly and harshly. 'I know it's not like they have at the farm. But I got what I could afford. He's used to meat, Stephen said, didn't you, Stephen? Why not get him what he's used to, to welcome him back, like. You ask Stephen how often we have meat in the normal run of things.'

Stephen, stolidly chewing, did not raise his head from his plate.

'I'll have it if he doesn't want it,' he said.

Enoch pushed his plate across the table, his face burning with shame.

After tea Stephen went out without saying where he was going, but Enoch guessed it was to meet Harold.

'Don't be late back,' said his mother. 'You have to be up for Sunday school in the morning.'

She made no attempt to talk to Enoch. He sat and watched her making bread, kneading the dough with strong, angry fingers. He felt completely in the way. At last he wandered out into the yard. He stood looking down the street to the corner where he used to find Polly. He was there until bedtime, listening to the noise of babies and drunken men, and watching the moon rise like a flare in the hazy sky. There was no one left to care for him, and it hurt too much for tears. 'Polly,' he whispered. 'Why did you go without a word?'

14

Stephen's story

Mam was always tired. She came home from her twelve hour shift at the terracotta factory exhausted, with barely enough energy to slice a loaf. Talking seemed to irritate her more than anything. Enoch quickly learnt to be as silent as Stephen when his mother was in the house. He learnt from Stephen, too, to share in the work. They got their own breakfast after their mother had left for work, and they did whatever they could towards the evening meal before she came home. Slowly Enoch grew used to the routine of gruel and potatoes and silence. There was no news of Polly. At school he searched the wall maps so hungrily that they imprinted his dreams. In a strange city with giant letters inked across its sky, he dreamed that Polly was hugging him.

There were, of course, no hugs outside his dreams. Stephen's friendliness was the only warmth in that bare house. Lonely as Enoch was, he could not keep up his defences against his brother. In bed, lying in the companionable dark, the two boys began to get to know each other. They began to put the pieces of their family together. Enoch spoke about Daniel, and Stephen talked about his life with Auntie Irene.

'I don't remember how I got sent there. I just remember knowing I wasn't theirs. Uncle Matthew went on about it sometimes, how they'd taken me in out of kindness. Not that I ever saw any. Saturdays were worst. They both got drunk on Saturdays. I just tried to keep their two little ones out of the way. That's all they wanted me for, to mind their little girls for them. There was no chance of school, though they packed us off to church every Sunday, out of the way. I can remember wondering if the workhouse would be better.'

'You must have been so lonely.'

Stephen nodded.

'That's why I feel different from you about Mam, Enoch. She wasn't like you describe. She used to come and visit me when she could. She'd just sit and hold my hand and cry and cry. She knew what was going on, but what could she do? She couldn't keep me. When she fetched me back, I didn't know she had sent you away instead. But I don't think it was that bad on the farm.'

'No,' said Enoch. 'No, it was fine. I'm glad she took you back, Stephen.' His old jealousy seemed a shameful thing, and yet it made him feel strange inside to know how she had cried over Stephen, how she had visited him.

'Mam loves you,' he said aloud. 'I don't think she loves me. She sees something in me – I don't know what it is.'

'Daniel loved you,' said Stephen. 'And Grandad.'

'But they're dead,' said Enoch bleakly. 'And I don't know how to find Polly.' Stephen was silent.

'Uncle Matthew used to talk about Polly in a horrible sort of way,' he said eventually. 'As if – as if she wasn't someone to be proud of in your family.'

'I love Polly,' said Enoch fiercely. 'I hardly ever see her, but when I do it's different from Daniel or Grandad or you. We don't have to speak. It doesn't matter if years have passed. We fit.'

'So where is Polly?' Stephen demanded. He sounded envious.

'I don't know,' said Enoch miserably. 'I wish I did.'

Stephen thought for a little while.

'Someone must know. Someone in the family, or one of the neighbours that knew her. Mr Dawson seems to know nearly everything. Maybe you should ask him.'

'Maybe.' Enoch wasn't so sure. He still felt shy of Mr Dawson. He hadn't seen him all the time he lived at the farm. Not that Mr Dawson appeared to hold it against him. He welcomed Enoch when he rejoined the Sunday school, and said something kind to him about Grandad. But Enoch suspected he wasn't the sort of grown-up who would treat a child seriously. When he came to talk to the Sunday school children, he always put on a specially bright voice, quite unlike the way he talked to adults.

Enoch was puzzled about something else.

'Why did Mam send you away and not me when our Dad died?'

'You were the youngest,' said Stephen. 'And anyway, Auntie Irene said there was no chance of anyone wanting to take you in, because –' he broke off.

'Because what?' Enoch demanded sharply.

'Nothing,' Stephen muttered. 'It was just some rubbish Auntie Irene said after she'd been at the bottle.'

'I need to know,' Enoch said urgently. 'You've got to tell me Stephen.'

Stephen sighed.

'All right,' he said. 'Only don't get angry with me. Auntie Irene said you were a – bastard. A little bastard, that's what she said. And then she passed out drunk, and I put the girls to bed.'

'A bastard,' Enoch said wonderingly. 'Do you think she meant I was horrible, or the other kind –'

'Don't know.' Stephen was gruff, as if he was embarrassed.

'I'm sick of being told I'm horrible. Mam and Uncle Stephen and Harold said it over and over.'

It came out of Enoch involuntarily, in an un-expected rush of feeling.

'You're not,' Stephen turned to him. His voice was matter of fact. 'I've seen enough horrible to know, Enoch. Trust me. If you're the other kind –' he paused. 'Well, I don't see whose bastard you'd be, really.' He gave a huge yawn. 'I'm tired now. It's time we were asleep.'

He turned on his side. Sleep always came easily to Stephen. Soon he was breathing deeply, curled away from Enoch. Enoch put a hand out and gently touched his brother's back. All his jealousy, all his fear of Stephen had melted away.

'My brother,' he said aloud.

15

A slip of the tongue

It was an evening in September, and Enoch had been back at his mother's house for three months. He was sitting in the kitchen reading an old storybook that Grandad had given him. There was no one here to talk to about what he read. Neither Mam nor Stephen had any interest in books. But when he read the old books, Enoch could remember Grandad's voice. At school he had moved up a standard, but there was no one at home to share his excitement, his pleasure at learning something new. In his head he spoke to Grandad, and, sometimes, to Daniel. Daniel seemed so far away now, on the very edge of memory. Mam would never talk about those days. And of course, she never mentioned Polly. Enoch ached to have news of her. On his way to school and back, he searched the streets for her. When he was up on the common with Stephen and Matthew, he would stop to watch the carts pass on the road below. One of them might bring her back. She would come back to him. He would not give up hope.

Soon after talking to Stephen, he went to see Mrs Liverstitch, now housebound with arthritis. Her face lit up when she saw him, but she could tell him very little.

'I know Polly went up to the farm to see you, once I told her you were there. And she used to leave letters for your grandfather to find, poor soul. But she didn't come and see me before she left, Enoch. It was such a sudden thing. Quite a shock. I hope she came to no harm, going off like that.'

'You haven't heard from her since she went away?' Enoch pleaded.

Mrs Liverstitch shook her head.

'I'm surprised she left without coming to the farm, or leaving you word. She cared so much for you, Enoch.'

He did not know who else to ask. That night, when Stephen was asleep, he took out the tin box that held everything he had from Polly. The little mouse and its sugar twin lay curled up with the notes in Polly's writing. He touched them gently. He still held on to

Polly's promise. She would come back one day.

It was almost too dark in the kitchen now for Enoch to see the words of his book. He got up to light the lamp. Outside in the street the women began to call their children in. The sky was dark blue, and clear enough tonight for the first star to be visible. Enoch went out to the scullery door and stood in the cooler air. Stephen would be home soon. He liked a cup of tea before going to bed. Enoch went back inside and put the kettle on to boil. When he sat down again, waiting for Stephen, he felt a little empty. The kitchen, which had seemed peaceful when the street was full of human noise, now seemed a lonely place. He almost welcomed the noise of floorboards creaking overhead, and the sound of his mother's steps on the stairs.

She came into the room with her head wrapped in a shawl, her hand pressed over one eye. She looked at him in some confusion.

'I thought I heard Stephen coming in.'

'No. Just me,' said Enoch. 'Do you want some tea? I was going to make some fresh for Stephen.'

She grunted, making for her chair and sitting down with a sharp intake of breath.

To his surprise, Enoch felt his guard lowering. Mam looked so frail and old in her ragged flannel petticoat. Something like pity came into his heart.

'That headache still bad, is it?'

'Just make that tea, can you?' she muttered, hugging herself tightly, as if there was no one else to hug her.

Enoch got busy with the teapot. He made her a strong black cup with extra sugar, how he knew she liked it. When he brought it, she closed her hands on it gratefully, murmuring thanks. He sat down at the table and drank his own in a silence that was unusually comfortable. Not to break it, but to draw closer to her, he said, 'I am glad to be back, Mam.'

She grunted.

'I like being here with Stephen,' Enoch added. 'It's funny, isn't it, that this is the first time we've lived together, all three of us?'

'It's what happens,' his mother said flatly. 'If you have money, it's easy to keep your family together. If not –' she shrugged and drank her tea. It seemed to revive her, because she turned slightly towards him.

'If you'd been earning something towards your keep you could have stayed here instead of going to the farm.'

'Really?'

A strange relief flooded through Enoch. Was that the only reason she had sent him away?

'You had Stephen back, though,' he said cautiously.

'Stephen was old enough for school. You needed minding. Wouldn't have happened in my day. I was minding the baby when I was four. At five I went to work.'

'You never went to school?' Enoch was startled.

'What's the use of school for working people?' she retorted roughly. 'What's the use of all those books you're so fond of? They don't tell you how to earn your bread or please the Lord. I learnt all I know at Sunday school. Six days a week in the fields, scaring crows, and one blessed day of rest.'

She was silent a moment, remembering.

'I used to eat my dinner in the field when I was working. Sometimes, in the summer, I would see a pony cart pass by on the road. That was the doctor's cart, and often his little girl was with him. I used to pretend it was me. Me, up in a pony cart, in a pretty dress, holding a doll. That was all the playing I had time for. I never had a real doll.'

Enoch could hardly bear it.

'When I grow up,' he said, 'you won't have to work any more. I'll go to work and bring all the money home, and you can have all of it. You can buy whatever you want.'

'Too late for a doll,' his mother said. 'I'd look funny with a doll, at my age.'

Her eyes were bright with tears.

Enoch got up and went towards her.

'But you can have lots of other nice things,' he said. 'I'm going to make sure of it. I'm not a bastard. I'm a good boy, and I'll prove it.'

'What did you say?'

Her anger hit him like a fist. He stepped back in shock.

'I said – lots of nice things. When I'm a grown-up.'

'The other bit. That word. Bastard, you said. Where did you get that from? Who've you been talking to?'

'No one,' Enoch lied. He was scared. He should have remembered, it was never safe to talk to Mam. Traps opened under your feet and you landed in Hell. She was getting up. Slowly, with a horrible effort, she was pulling herself to her feet. Enoch began to back away.

'Have you been in touch with Polly?'

'No!'

Her hand whipped out of her shawl and grabbed him, pulling him back to her.

'I don't trust you. You used to see her before, didn't you? Even though I told you I didn't like it. So how do I know you're telling me the truth?'

'I am, Mam. I promise,' he gabbled, afraid of the look in her eyes.

Her hands gripped his shoulders and shook him hard.

'You'd better be telling me the truth. You'd better not be lying.'

Enoch shut his eyes and prayed for her to stop.

'I'm not lying. Of course I'm not. I'm a good boy, I am,' he gasped out.

'I hope so,' said his mother, letting go suddenly. 'I hope you are. I see you watching me, Enoch, staring and thinking. Children aren't meant to think. They're meant to do as they're told. It'd be better for you if you were more like Stephen. I never have to worry about what's going on in his head.'

'Is that why you like him better than me?' Enoch asked.

He couldn't help asking, though her outraged face told him it was a mistake.

'There you go again. Questions, always questions! When does Stephen come asking questions? He's a good honest lad, for all he's a bit slow. He doesn't need keeping on the straight and narrow. None of my sons ever did.'

There was a moment of appalling silence. He knew what she had said, and so did she. He saw a shiver go through her, and then a terrible rage sweep over her face. She pushed him down so he was kneeling at her feet.

'We're going to pray,' she said harshly. 'Pray for

your delivery from curiosity and pride in your cleverness. We're going to pray to have the sin of your conceiving driven out of you.'

Her voice rose, drunk on fury and righteousness, as she poured out her demands to the Almighty. He began to pray too with all his heart, sobbing in fear and confusion. When her hard red hands began to beat God into him there seemed no reason why she should ever stop. Under the storm of her fists, he felt himself collapsing, reduced to nothing, but at the core of him there was now a saving grace. This was not his mother. He was free of her.

16

The whole world
before him

Stephen's voice came from the doorway, low and hesitant.

'Shall I bring you a cup of tea?'

Enoch opened his eyes. His brother's words repeated themselves in his head. He managed a nod and settled back against the pillows as Stephen's feet rattled down the stairs. Then tears began to squeeze out of his eyes and slide over his swollen face onto the pillow. He lay without moving until Stephen returned.

'Where's Mam?' he asked Stephen hoarsely.

'She's gone to work already.'

Stephen held the cup while Enoch slowly pushed himself upright. He watched Enoch drink the scalding black tea thirstily.

'She's never beaten me like that. When I came in last night and heard it –'

'She only stopped because you were there,' Enoch said. 'I don't think she knew how to stop otherwise.'

Stephen looked distressed.

'I've never seen her like that before. I know you said about – about how she was when you were little. But I thought, maybe you'd remembered wrong. I've been feeling a bit jealous, Enoch. I thought maybe she liked you better, for being clever and that. And now this –' he reached a gentle hand towards Enoch's bruised face.

'She hates me,' Enoch said. The hands holding his cup started to shake. 'I'm not hers, that's why. She told me so, Stephen. So why did she bother to keep me at all?'

Stephen took the cup off him.

'I don't believe it,' he said doggedly. 'Look at you. Anyone can see we must be brothers.'

'She kept going on about my sins,' said Enoch, the tears springing into his eyes again. 'Last night. You heard her. She kept saying that sin had been bred into me, and nothing would get it out.'

'It's her,' Stephen said. He stroked his brother's hair. 'It's just her. She's got that side to her. It comes out at her Bible meetings and all. Sometimes I think she's bit mad. You say your prayers, don't you, same as me? When I get into fights, she doesn't say it's the devil, she says it's me. You're no different. Ask Mr Dawson if you don't believe me. He'll tell you. Ask Mrs Liverstitch that's so fond of you.'

Enoch shook his head as if nothing could make a difference, but when Stephen handed back his tea his hands were steady.

'Are you coming to school, or will you stop here?'

Enoch lay down again and pulled the blankets up to his chin.

'I'll stop here.'

Stephen nodded.

'That's best. You've got two black eyes. Samson's bound to ask where you got them.'

'Don't tell him,' Enoch said anxiously.

Stephen smiled.

'I'll tell him you're ill in bed. That's no lie.'

Enoch slept. When he woke again, he heard the church clock chiming. It was twelve o'clock. Midday. He lay quietly, no less sore, but with a clear mind. If he wasn't Mam's, then she had no right to beat him. He was sure of that, as sure as if he had seen it written in the Bible. If he wasn't Mam's, he was free to go. But where could he go, and who would take him in? Mam's hard hands had marked him as something bad, something unwanted.

'Auntie May won't take me back,' he whispered. 'Uncle Stephen won't let her. Mrs Liverstitch is ill and old. I'd only be a nuisance to her. I'd run away to Polly, if only I knew where she was.'

Then he remembered what Stephen had said. He would go and see Mr Dawson. Mr Dawson was an educated man. Mr Dawson would know what he should do.

It took a painful effort to creep out of bed and ease on his clothes. He shuffled himself down the stairs and out, at the pace of an arthritic old man. When he got to the vicarage, he stood on the step for a full minute before he found the courage to ring the bell. And when the housemaid came to answer it, he wished he hadn't. She looked him up and down, her lips sucked in with disapproval.

'Well, you might have washed your face before you came out. Is this your first day on the job or what? Delivery boys have to go straight round the back.'

'I'm not delivering. I want to see him.'

'Him? Who's him?'

'Mr Dawson,' said Enoch faintly.

'I don't know why he should see some young hooligan that's just been in a fight. Anyway, he's not at home, so you can't. Mrs Dawson is in at present, but she's going out later, so you can't see her either.'

'I'll wait,' said Enoch. 'I'll wait till he comes back. I'll wait here on the doorstep, or inside. I don't mind. I'm not going till I've seen him.'

'Well, we'll see what Mrs Dawson will have to say about that,' the girl said sharply.

She shut the door on him, and he heard her footsteps clacking down the hall. Enoch shut his eyes and leant against the porch. He wondered exactly what the girl was telling Mrs Dawson, whom he hardly knew. Mr Dawson had married her while he was at the farm and not going to church. Enoch just hoped she wouldn't shout at him. He was too raw inside to bear it.

In a minute the maid returned, looking grumpy.

'She says she'll see you herself.' She tossed her dark head under her cap. 'It wouldn't be what I'd do, but there we are.'

Enoch opened his mouth to say he didn't want to see Mrs Dawson, but his courage deserted him. He meekly followed the housemaid down the carpeted hall.

'In you go.'

She opened the door of a large square room.

'Mind you don't touch anything, and I hope you wiped your boots. Mrs Dawson'll be along presently.'

Enoch was left standing near the door. He had never been inside the vicarage before. The first thing he noticed were the books. There were two big glass-fronted bookcases running from floor to ceiling, crammed full. He wanted to go over and look at them, but he was afraid to move from the spot. Near the window there was a big black desk with a writing stand and paper and more books. Enoch guessed that was where Mr Dawson wrote his sermons. There was a fire in the fireplace, laid but unlit, with an armchair drawn up close by. He hadn't time to notice anything more, because Mrs Dawson came in behind him.

'I'm sorry Mr Dawson isn't here. Perhaps I can help you instead?'

Enoch turned round, startled by the gentleness in her voice. He remembered how quiet, almost shy she had been on her visits to Sunday school. She was small and slight, with light brown curly hair. Too thin, Mam said. Likely to be carried off with her first baby. But her first baby was nearly two now, and she was still here. She stood gazing at him with steady patience, while he looked down at the hem of her plum-coloured dress and smelt the clean flowery smell she had. He wished to answer her, but no words came. She was so gentle, so soft looking. How could he talk to her about what Mam had done?

'Is somebody ill? Would you like to leave a message for Mr Dawson?'

The front door banged shut, and there was a noise of voices in the hall.

'Oh, there's John,' said Mrs Dawson with relief. 'I'll just go and say you're here.'

She disappeared quickly, and it was Mr Dawson who re-entered the room.

'Now then, Enoch,' he said briskly, walking over to the desk and standing with his back to it. 'What's this all about?'

His hands grasped the edge of the desk, and he tapped his foot slightly.

Enoch did not know how to begin. His fingers shredded the torn lining of his cap.

'I came to tell you that I'm leaving home,' he said at last in a voice that sounded much bolder than he felt. 'I want to find my sister. I thought you would know how I could go about it.'

Mr Dawson's foot stopped tapping. He looked surprised, and more than a little amused.

'I see.' His voice sounded the way it did when someone gave a silly answer in Sunday school. 'You're a little young to be wanting your independence. You haven't been home with your mother more than a couple of months. Much better to stay where you are and get used to it than to go off somewhere else, don't you think? Your mother is a fine Christian woman,

Enoch, and you are very lucky to have a fine Christian home –'

To his fierce shame, Enoch began crying.

'Oh come now, Enoch, come now,' murmured Mr Dawson, pulling out his handkerchief and handing it over. As Enoch took it blindly and began to wipe his face, Mr Dawson said in different voice, a sharp one: 'Did she give you those marks on your face?'

Enoch nodded.

'But she isn't my mother,' he said. 'That's why I'm leaving.'

Mr Dawson was speechless.

'Did your – did Mrs Kirk tell you that?' he managed at last.

Enoch hesitated.

'She didn't mean to. But I found it out.'

'I see.'

Mr Dawson reached forward and touched Enoch's face gingerly.

'This is appalling,' he muttered. 'Really, this is very shocking.'

His sympathy gave Enoch the courage to ask a question that really scared him.

'Mr Dawson, is my real mother someone very bad? Is that why Mam says sin is bred into me?'

The clergyman looked flustered.

'I – well, I really think that's something you'll have to take up with your – with Mrs Kirk.'

Enoch nodded. He was almost relieved not to know. He could not see how it would be good news.

He offered Mr Dawson back his handkerchief, and the vicar took the sodden ball gingerly and laid it on the desk.

'You're a good boy, Enoch,' he said, rather to his own surprise. 'A lucky boy, too. If I was you, I'd stay at home quietly, and not go looking for your sister or anyone else. You'll need to work hard to justify your grandfather's plans for you.'

Enoch looked at him. He felt a flare of anger.

'My Grandad's dead,' he said sharply. 'What plans could he have for me?'

Mr Dawson fiddled awkwardly with the change in his pockets.

'I'm surprised Mrs Kirk hasn't told you. Your grandfather left a sum of money in trust for your education. He wished you to study theology.'

Enoch's face lit up with surprise and delight. 'To be a vicar like you? Grandad, Grandad, thank you!'

He felt as though a rope had been lowered down to him from heaven. It didn't matter if Mam hit him. He was not forsaken.

'I suppose that's why Uncle Stephen was so angry

159

at the funeral. I got the money he thought should have gone to him.'

He looked over at the bookcase longingly.

'Does it mean I'll get some new books soon? I've read all the ones Grandad gave me so many times.'

Mr Dawson smiled.

'Plenty of books,' he said, 'when the time comes. You're still at elementary school, aren't you?'

Enoch nodded.

'But I want to get started. I'm clever, Mr Dawson. And you don't know how hard I will work.'

'I think I'm beginning to understand what your grandfather saw in you, Enoch. When you finish school, come and see me again. I'll do my best to help.'

But Enoch felt the best help had already been given. Studying would be his escape from Mam.

'You can be a vicar anywhere, can't you, Mr Dawson? I wouldn't have to stay in Gresley?'

Mr Dawson smiled.

'You could be chaplain to a London mission, or go out to Africa or the South Seas. The whole world is open to you, Enoch.'

And somewhere in it, he would find Polly.

PART FOUR

'I don't know who I am!'

17

The Boy Wonder of Gresley

Once he knew about the money Grandad had left to him, Enoch gave all his mind to getting through elementary school. He passed the leavers' standard at only ten years old. For a while it was the talk of the neighborhood, eclipsing even the fire at number forty and the Dawsons' new baby boy. Proudly, Enoch went with Stephen to tell Mrs Liverstitch. She took his hand and there were tears in her eyes.

'You always were a clever lad. I'll never forget Daniel showing me your writing on that slate of his. He's up in heaven now, enjoying your triumph.'

'Really?'

Mrs Liverstitch nodded. 'And your Grandad. They

can see all that happens. If only Polly was here to see it too.'

'I'll find her,' Enoch said. 'You know I'm going to find her one day.'

'I hope so, lad,' said Mrs Liverstitch. But there was little hope in her expression as she said it. Her face brightened as she went on. 'You were such a funny little thing when Daniel had you. You promised you'd teach me to read, remember?'

'I will. Of course I will!' Enoch told her. 'We can start whenever you like.'

But Mrs Liverstitch shook her head.

'I'm too old now, love. Too old and too stupid. For every new thing I learn, I forget two old ones. It's too late for me, but I shall enjoy seeing you get on. When you're a bishop all dressed in purple and gold, I shall look up at you in the pulpit while you're thundering away at us, and I shall think –'

'You'll think how you wiped his snotty nose when he was little,' said Stephen with a grin.

Enoch didn't mind Stephen's teasing. He knew Stephen was proud of him.

'My belief is you'll end up a bishop,' Mrs Liverstitch said happily. 'I couldn't believe it when your Mam told me about your legacy. At last, a bit of good fortune. You make the most of it, Enoch. It's the first to come your family's way in a long time. I expect your Mam is very proud of you.'

Enoch glanced at Stephen.

'She's not proud of me. She's never proud of me, whatever I do. But I don't care, because I didn't do it for her, I did it for Grandad.'

Mrs Liverstitch shook her head. 'That's not the way to talk about your Mam, Enoch. She's done her best for you, though it may be hard for you to see it.'

Enoch bit his lip stubbornly, but his fondness for Mrs Liverstitch prevented him from saying any more.

After they left, Stephen said:

'It's not true to say Mam isn't proud of you, Enoch. She just can't find ways to show it, that's all.'

'She hates me!' Enoch said, his face blazing with passion. 'Oh, she doesn't belt me like she used to, not since Mr Dawson spoke to her. She just ignores me. Haven't you noticed, Stephen? She doesn't even look at me if she can help it. And when we came back from school, and you told her and showed her my prize book, what did she say?'

'She said not to let it go to your head,' Stephen said unwillingly. 'All right, she'd have said more if it was me, I admit it. Now, please can we go and meet Matthew? It's not often he has a half day, now he's working up at Green's Pottery.'

They spent the afternoon on the common with Matthew, fishing for minnows in the cold rushing stream.

'Do you remember how I used to creep about up here spying for you, Enoch?' Matthew said with a grin.

Enoch nodded, embarrassed.

'It drove Harold nearly round the bend,' said Stephen, giving his brother a thump on the arm. 'I saw Harold the other day. He didn't want to stop and talk to me. I suppose he thinks he's too grand now he's left school and I'm still there.'

Enoch was holding his jam jar of minnows up to the light.

'They always die, poor little things,' he said. 'It doesn't matter if you add water weed or anything. Why don't we just put them back in the stream?'

The other boys looked at him in horror.

'You must be joking, after all the trouble we've had catching 'em!' said Matthew. 'Their life's not bad. They have a better time than us, if you think about it. No work for them. They just swim round and round.'

Enoch laughed. He thought working suited Matthew. There was a confident look on his face he had never worn in school. He was beginning to put on weight, and his working clothes were less ragged than his old school jumper.

'I thought you liked work,' Stephen said, looking a little anxious. He too would be starting work in a year or so.

'I like the money,' said Matthew. He jingled his pocket. 'My granny lets me keep sixpence out of my wages. I'll buy us some sweets on the way home.'

'Anyway, there'll be no work for you, Enoch,' said Stephen. 'Didn't Mr Dawson say you should be sent to some fancy school?'

Enoch shook his head. 'He said he should speak to Mam first.' He was afraid to talk about it, afraid even to hope. What if, after all, something should go wrong?

Mam was late back from work, and when at last she came home, she looked more than usually exhausted.

'I went to see that Mr Dawson of yours,' she announced to Enoch as she flopped into a chair. 'First of all I had to sit through a long sermon about the benefits of education. When at last he got to the point, it turns out that he doesn't know what to do with you. The county college doesn't take boys under fifteen, and none of the private schools will have a boy from the working class.'

Enoch did not want her to see his disappointment. He got up and began to make the tea. As he poured the boiling water into the pot, his hand shook a little and he scalded himself. It hurt, but not as much as he felt inside.

'So what's going to happen?' Stephen asked.

'Well, I said, "Fine, he can go to work instead." But Mr Dawson wasn't happy about that. He said it was a waste of talent. "I'll tutor him myself," he said, "but I can only spare a few hours a week." "All right," I told him, "you do that, but for the rest of the time he can go out to work. That'll cover the cost of feeding him, which is more than your precious educating is worth."'

Enoch carried the teapot carefully to the table.

'So I'm going to have lessons with Mr Dawson?' he said. His voice was controlled, but he could not help smiling.

'You are,' said Mam. 'And I shall go down to Green's Pottery tomorrow and ask about a job for you. I expect they'll take you on as a half-timer. About time you started bringing something into this house.'

Enoch picked up his prize schoolbook and pretended to read it. Nothing Mam said could trouble him, so long as his lessons were settled. Her bitterness couldn't touch him.

'He's not even listening,' Mam complained to Stephen. 'What possessed that man to leave the money all in a lump to him, instead of sharing it out among all of us –'

'Don't go on, Mam,' said Stephen uncomfortably. 'What's it matter?'

'Matter! It was enough to buy you decent dinners, and a new set of clothes now and then.'

Stephen thought about it for a moment, eyes gleaming. Then, with an effort, he shook his head.

'No, I'm happy for Enoch to get his chance. I'll be stuck in Gresley all my life, but he's got the brains to make something of himself.'

'Thank you, Stephen,' Enoch said, smiling at his brother. He didn't even glance at Mam before turning back to his book. Never mind about having to work. He was glad it would be Mr Dawson teaching him. He thought of all the books in those glass-fronted bookcases. He couldn't wait to begin.

His job at Green's started first, though. It was ten to six on a Monday morning when Enoch walked through the front gates of Green's Pottery and stared around the yard. Men and boys pushed past him, surly and hunched against the start of another working week. Immediately ahead rose imposing three storey building with a rickety wooden staircase winding round it. Enoch recognised the swelling belly of an oven, but what did the saggar house look like? He began to walk past piles of crates and massive bales of hay, picking his way through the yard, which was scattered about with broken crates and bits of old rope, deposits of clay and scattered nuggets of coke. Already there were crashing noises of men at work. Somewhere someone was whistling. He peered in at a doorway, and was cursed by a boy setting off at a run on some errand.

'Saggar house?' Enoch asked. In the semi-darkness he could see men and odd shaped machines.

'Does this look like a sodding saggar house?' someone shouted.

'Next building across the yard,' said a milder voice.

It was an extraordinary noise, a kind of thumping, regular and heavy. At first it seemed almost continuous, then, as Enoch stepped into the poorly lit shed, it resolved itself into about a dozen separate rhythms. When his eyes adjusted he saw the place was already full of men and boys, beating out fireclay. Many were already stripped to the waist. Without pause, tirelessly it seemed, the men raised the big mallets and brought them smashing down on the clay. But the nearest boy caught Enoch's eye. He was already struggling, stopping frequently to get his breath and wipe away the sweat. His arms look thin and weak, and as he turned to cough, Enoch saw the desperate look on his face.

'I'm looking for Isaac Clamp,' Enoch shouted to him. Without bothering to speak, the boy gestured with his thumb towards a wiry man with a heavily muscled neck and shoulders. He was clean-shaven, and his wispy grey hair was already speckled with clay. As Enoch walked over to him, he had a mallet raised above his head. He brought it smacking down into the clay, took his hands from it and let it stick. He looked Enoch over, his face calm and intelligent.

'Are you Ellen Kirk's lad, then? The sharp one that can't stop at school?'

Enoch nodded.

'I thought maybe you weren't coming. We start at six on this shift.' He spoke so quietly that Enoch could only follow his words from the movement of his lips.

'I know,' Enoch bellowed, still fighting the noise. 'I couldn't find this place.'

'Never mind.' With a curious twist of his neck, Isaac put both fault and excuse behind him. 'Take off your coat, and your shirt too, if you've sense, and I'll show you what to do. There are pegs over on that wall.'

Enoch did as he was told. The saggar house was cold, and he felt chilly and self-conscious. As he walked back he noticed that most of the boys were working in bare feet, and that their trousers were stiff with clay. He had felt uncomfortable wearing his oldest trousers, patched at the crotch and much too short, but now he was glad. Mam had been right. There was no point in looking smart for the saggar house.

Isaac, meanwhile, had been studying his movements with a concentrated frown.

'You're a well-grown lad,' he mouthed. 'And you don't look clumsy. Anyhow, I'll show you what to do.'

He placed Enoch at the brick table in front of him, and put the wooden mallet, which he called a mow, into Enoch's hands. On the table there was an iron hoop with a great lump of fireclay in it. It was half-flattened already. Enoch set to, trying to beat out the clay so that it lay flat within the hoop. He was aware of Isaac watching him critically, so he put all his strength into the blows. After ten or fifteen minutes he was sweating and exhausted. The mow kept slipping in his wet palms, and he could hardly keep lifting it straight above his head, let alone bring it down with any force. When it landed in the clay it got stuck, and he had to stop and prise it out. At last, as he lifted the mow up, Isaac caught and held it, and took it out of his trembling fingers.

'I can learn it,' Enoch gasped. He did not want to

have to go home and tell Mam he had been turned off on his first day.

'Yes, I think you can,' said Isaac.

Enoch looked at him gratefully.

'Just let the mow fall when you've swung it up,' Isaac told him. 'No need to bang it down. Get a good rhythm going, and gravity'll provide the force your little arms can't.'

He swung up the mow and handed it back. 'Finish it when you've rested.'

In the time it took Enoch to get his breath fully under control and for the hot pain in his shoulders to subside into a dull ache, Isaac had beaten out a large sheet of fireclay on another table. Enoch watched him cut out a piece of the clay and begin wrapping it round a wooden drum. Then he took up his mow again. He stopped at last, thinking he had finished. The clay was lumpy and humped on one side, but it filled the hoop. Gently, Isaac nudged him aside, and flattened and smoothed the clay with a few blows.

'Now you'll see what the thing's for.'

Carefully he lifted the circle of clay and fixed it on top of the round shape he had made.

'When it's fired, it'll be a saggar,' Isaac said.

Enoch knew this already from talking to Matthew

about his work, but he nodded, gingerly touching his shoulders with his fingers.

'All the ware, when it comes to be fired, goes into a saggar bedded with flint. That's so the ware will keep its shape. The saggars are stacked up in the hovel – you know, the oven – with the green ones. Like this one, on top, because they can't bear any weight until they've been fired themselves. Now you take this along to the drying house across the yard, and when you come back, there'll be another lump of clay for you to wreck.'

He said this with such a grin that Enoch did not feel hurt.

But it took all his strength to heave the saggar out into the yard. The cold spring air and the light dazzled him; he shivered as the wind struck his bare skin, but he had no time to run back for his coat. He lurched off in the direction of the drying house. There was a bottle of cold tea and a hunk of bread in his coat pocket. His mouth was dry and he was weak with hunger and effort, but it would be an hour before he could have breakfast, and then the bulk of the shift was still ahead of him. Six days a week, he remembered, as he ran back, shivering, to the saggar house. If it weren't for Grandad's money, this would be his life. This was Matthew's life. This would be Stephen's.

Guiltily, he wondered how they could bear it.

At the end of the shift, he could hardly stand. His arms and legs shook, and he needed Isaac's help to put on his shirt again.

'It's always like this at the start,' Isaac comforted him. 'You'll harden to it. Get your Mam to rub your back and sponge you down with hot water. It'll stop you being so stiff in the morning.'

Enoch was too tired to do anything but nod. He crept home, and into bed, and slept until Stephen woke him, coming in from school.

It was Stephen he got to massage his neck and shoulders in the evening. Mam went early to bed, so they had a good time, laughing together at Enoch's exaggerated howls of agony.

'I'm jealous of all this half-time working,' Stephen joked. 'You'll have iron muscles by Christmas. I won't dare cross you or you'll knock me flat.'

'I'll look forward to that,' Enoch said, pulling his nightshirt on. 'Seriously, though, I'll help you when it's your turn.'

'You'd better,' said Stephen. 'Although you'll probably be a bishop in Africa by the time they let me out of school. I finished bottom of the class again last week. Mr Samson caned me out of sheer despair.'

'Do you hate it?' Enoch asked suddenly. He'd loved

school so much, he'd never wondered how it felt to be no good at it.

'I'll hate work more,' Stephen answered philosophically. 'But at least there's money in that. How much are you getting?'

'Three shillings a week,' said Enoch. 'Well, Mam is.'

'She'll give you tuppence back to put in your pocket, I expect,' said Stephen. 'Then I can start charging you for back rubs. See, I knew there was something in it for me.'

Next morning Enoch had to leave the house before Stephen was even awake. He shuffled along as quickly as his stiff legs would go, afraid of being late a second day. Just as he reached gates of the pottery, he saw a group of boys waiting outside. He knew at once what was going to happen.

'Look who's here!'

'It's the Boy Wonder!'

'How's your private lessons going, professor?'

They were all bigger than him, and worked the full shift like men. Enoch knew he should be scared, but instead he felt angry.

'You can knock me down if you like,' he said to the nearest, a lad of thirteen called Henry Spilling. 'It won't make your brains any bigger.'

The others sniggered and glanced at Henry, and

Enoch realised he had made a mistake. Henry Spilling scowled. 'You think yourself so clever, don't you? You think you're better than all the rest of us.'

'I don't,' said Enoch.

But the other boys, picking up their signal, had crowded in.

'Tell your big brother he brags too much,' said Henry Spilling. 'I've been hearing too much about you. About how clever you are, and about your money, and how you're going to end up in a pulpit somewhere, looking down on the likes of us. Well, you're still down in the dirt with us now, so don't you forget it. And if I want you to lick my dirty boots clean, I can make you, see?'

They let Henry land the first punch. Then they were all on him. He fell to the ground with them on top, but there were too many of them trying for them to really hurt him. Henry saw this and yelled at them to get up. He got a couple of his lads to hold Enoch down, while the others started kicking him. Now Enoch was scared. He heard the men walking in through the gate, cursing the boys out of the way, but no one stopped to help. He took a couple of bad kicks to his legs and his back. Then he heard an angry yell, and suddenly no one was holding him. The boys were gone. A strong arm helped him to his feet, and gently patted him down.

'Nothing broken,' said a familiar voice.

It was Matthew.

Enoch felt tears start up in his eyes, and brushed his sleeve over his face, ashamed to be seen crying. But Matthew was unconcerned.

'You're shaken, it's only natural.'

He took Enoch's arm and began to walk with him into the yard.

'I looked out for you yesterday. I would have called for you at home if you'd asked me.'

Enoch felt the reproach underlying the gentle words.

'I'm sorry, Matthew. I've been thinking so hard about starting lessons with Mr Dawson, I haven't bothered much about this end of things. It's not as if I'll be working at Green's for ever.'

'Not like me, you mean,' said Matthew a little grimly. 'So when do you start with Mr Dawson?'

'I'm seeing him this afternoon. I hope he doesn't expect too much.'

'You'll be fine,' Matthew said. He grinned. 'When I closed my books on the last day at school I promised myself I'd never open another one, but I know you feel different.'

They reached the saggar house. Enoch let go of Matthew's arm.

'I have to go in here,' he said.

'Who are you working for?' Matthew asked. 'Isaac Clamp?'

Enoch nodded.

'He's a good 'un. Isaac won't cheat you, and he'll treat you right. My first master here was a swine.'

He gave Enoch a parting pat on the arm.

'Don't worry about Henry Spilling's lot,' he said. 'They pick on all the new lads. I'll call for you tomorrow, just so they get the message that you're friends with a big lad. And Enoch –' he looked at him hesitantly.

'Yes?'

'I know you'll be busier now, what with all your new studying and that. But don't forget old friends, hey? We've had some good times, you and me.'

Enoch nodded. 'I know. But I'll see you here every day, won't I? I don't know what I'll have time for outside work, though. I'm going to be really busy.'

Matthew thought a moment. 'What about this? On Saturday night, when I've got a bit of money in my pocket, we could walk over to Ashby and see the shops all lit up. There are hot meat pies almost as good as your Auntie used to make. I owe you a few, I reckon.'

Enoch nodded hungrily. 'That's a deal!'

All morning Enoch worried about his lesson with Mr Dawson. He found it difficult to concentrate; luckily Isaac put it down to tiredness.

'You'll harden to the work, lad,' he said kindly. 'All the young'uns find the first week tough.'

After his shift, Enoch just had time to limp home, wash in cold water and change into his Sunday clothes. At three o'clock the housemaid, with infinite disapproval, was showing him into Mr Dawson's study.

'Come in, come in,' said Mr Dawson, rubbing his hands with a nervous smile. He pointed to an extra chair drawn up beside his desk. 'Do sit down, and we'll make a start.'

Mr Dawson's clean soapy smell wafted over Enoch as he sat down. The vicar's collar gleamed immaculately above his sleek black coat. Enoch's own clothes felt clumsy and thick. He was hot and sweating with the effort of getting to his lesson. He shifted uncomfortably in his seat and one of his imperfectly cleaned boots touched Mr Dawson's trousers. The blood rushed into Enoch's face at thought he might have muddied them. He wished with all his heart he had not come.

Then, to his surprise, he realised that Mr Dawson too was ill at ease. He had three or four books in front of him, and he touched now one, then another, with his clean white fingers. He cleared his throat, hesitated, then finally spoke.

'Well, then, Enoch. I trust you are settling in at your new employment?'

Enoch nodded cautiously.

Mr Dawson seemed relieved.

'I have given some thought to a plan of study, though the materials to hand are hardly adapted to a child of your years. However –' He took a deep breath, and picked up the nearest book. 'This is Wayland's *Elements of Moral Science*. This will be our primer. You may read the first chapter out to me, and then we shall discuss it, smoothing out any difficulties. We will progress through the whole book, chapter by chapter, examining your understanding as we go, until by the end, you should have the whole in your mental possession. Then perhaps, if our lessons continue, we can proceed to more substantial works.'

Enoch nodded.

'I'm ready,' he said.

Mr Dawson settled the book on the desk in a convenient place between them. Enoch cleared his throat anxiously, leant forward in his chair and began to read in a hoarse rapid voice.

'Chapter First: Of the Origin of our Notion of the Moral Quality of Actions . . .' He read on, pausing to sound out the harder words, stumbling sometimes, and receiving corrections from Mr Dawson. Once Mr Dawson put a hand on his arm and stopped him altogether.

'Try to read it as though it had a meaning,' he said in a pained voice.

Light dawned on Enoch.

'You mean, read like I read to Grandad, not like they read at school?' he said excitedly.

Mr Dawson nodded in surprise, then pleasure as Enoch continued.

'That's just right,' he said. 'Just right.'

He sat back, a look of relief on his face.

Enoch read on, absorbed and exhilarated, an explorer of new worlds.

18

A daydream

'Coming to the Boys' Club with me tomorrow night?' Stephen said, as he hopped into bed.

He looked across the room, shaking his head a little, as if he still could not believe the changes. Enoch had done his best to turn the bedroom they shared into a version of Mr Dawson's study. He was sitting now at an old table Mrs Liverstitch had given him for a desk. Some cheap prints of Roman and Greek statues were tacked up on the walls above his head, and he had even found a bit of threadbare red carpet to cover the bare boards.

Enoch kept his eyes fixed on the book in front of him.

'I'm going round to the Dawsons',' he said reluctantly.

'What, again?'

'It's quieter,' Enoch said defensively. 'You know how much noise there is in the street on a Saturday night. And Mr Dawson has the books I need.'

Stephen looked troubled. Enoch spent much of his free time at the Dawsons these days.

'You know Mam doesn't like you being round there so much,' he said quietly. Enoch felt a hot flare of anger.

'I don't care. Evenings are my only chance to study, and the vicarage is the best place for it. If Mam can't understand a simple thing like that –'

Stephen was quiet for a moment, then he tried a different tack.

'When's the last time you went out with Matthew?'

Enoch looked sullen.

'Matthew knows I've a lot to do.'

'But you never make the effort to see him. He always has to come and look for you. Half the time when he does you're at the Dawsons and he's too shy to go there.'

Enoch shrugged indifferently. Matthew was a kind and faithful friend, but all they had in common now was Green's and the saggar house. Matthew couldn't talk about history and poetry, and he didn't understand when Enoch tried to talk to him.

'I know another reason why you go round to the Dawsons so much,' Stephen persisted.

Enoch stopped trying to read.

'Go on then,' he said tiredly.

'It's Mrs Dawson, isn't it? She makes you feel you belong there, not with us any more.'

Enoch shut his book with a bang.

'She's kind to me, yes,' he said. 'A lot kinder than the old cow we have to live with.'

'Don't call Mam an old cow!' Stephen said hotly.

'She may be your mam,' said Enoch, 'but I can call her anything I like, can't I, seeing she isn't mine?'

Stephen threw off the bedclothes and stood up.

'You're going to have to get this sorted out,' he said. 'Whoever your mother is, Mam's the one who's brought you up, and struggled to feed and keep you. Why do you think she bothered, if she doesn't care about you?'

Enoch shrugged off Stephen's arm.

'How should I know? But what she did for me, she did grudgingly. If I'd had only Mam to care for me, I'd have died inside long ago.'

'All right,' said Stephen, breathing hard. 'All right, but it's not only Mam I'm talking about. It's all your family, Enoch. When's the last time you talked to me about Polly? Have you forgotten how much she used to mean to you, and how much you wanted her back? The only people you care about these days are the Dawsons.'

Enoch shut his eyes. 'I still want to look for Polly,' he said. 'But I have to wait till I can get out of Gresley to do that. And sometimes I think, perhaps she's forgotten me. It's been so long since I heard from her. Maybe I should forget all about Polly, Stephen, and just make the best of what I've got now.'

'And that's the Dawsons, is it?'

Stephen's voice sounded hurt and angry.

Enoch simply shrugged. He didn't expect his brother to understand. He scarcely understood himself how, in a few short months, he had become so close to the Dawson family. It started when he wrote his first essay for Mr Dawson. His tutor took it from him gingerly, but as he began to read, his expression changed. He glanced from Enoch and back at the closely written pages.

'These are your own ideas, are they? Your own thoughts about the arguments in chapter seven?'

Enoch looked at him, confused.

'I mean, you didn't find them in a book, or get them from another person?'

'I only have the books you gave me, Mr Dawson. And there's only you I can talk to about what's in them.'

'Remarkable. Truly remarkable.' Mr Dawson stared at him for a long moment. 'I'd like you to stay for tea after today's lesson, Enoch. That's if you don't have to hurry home.'

Enoch was so scared that he nearly refused to stay, and when he saw the tea table he wished he had gone straight home. The china cups looked so delicate he was frightened to pick one up, and there was a napkin on his plate that he didn't know what to do with. He didn't dare eat anything except plain bread and butter, especially after he saw the way Mrs Dawson ate her cake with a fork. He was too scared to tell her he didn't want milk in his tea. She tried to talk to him about his family and about Sunday school, but he couldn't manage more than one syllable in reply. He saw her raise her eyebrows across the table at Mr Dawson, and caught his tutor's apologetic frown in reply. Blushing red, Enoch promised himself he would never, never stay to tea at the Dawsons' again.

Just then, Louisa Dawson, their four year old daughter, got down from her place at table and marched round to him.

'Cheer up, Enoch,' she said. 'Never mind the silly grown-ups. I'll get a jam tart for you. I know you want one, I saw you looking at them.'

'Louisa!' her mother cried out in horror.

But Louisa had stretched across the table and stuffed a jam tart into Enoch's mouth before anyone could stop her.

'I'll have one too,' she said, climbing on Enoch's lap to eat it. She patted Enoch's bulging cheeks, and felt her own.

'Good,' she announced indistinctly.

Simultaneously, they both exploded with laughter, sending a shower of jammy crumbs up over the table like a small volcano.

'Oh, Louisa!' said Mr Dawson.

His voice was stern, but he was trying not to laugh himself. Then somehow everyone was talking, and it was easy for Mrs Dawson to pass him things, and show him how to use his cutlery. Now when he stayed for tea, he had both children on his lap. Mr Dawson talked about books and Mrs Dawson talked about her own family, far away in Yorkshire. He felt at ease with them. He felt as if he belonged.

Stephen had got back into bed, and pulled the bedclothes up around him.

'You're so wrapped up in your precious Dawsons that you haven't noticed how things have changed here,' he persisted. 'Mam's changed. She believes in your studying now. She's proud of you.'

'She never shows it,' said Enoch sulkily.

'She's kept that bit of newspaper when they said about you preaching at Easter. You know, the "Boy Wonder of Gresley" article. She has it in that box of hers, along with her mourning brooch, and Daniel's baby shoes.'

'I didn't know that,' said Enoch. He looked at his brother.

'Do you really think she's proud of me?'

Stephen nodded.

'Well, it's a bit late now,' Enoch said despondently. 'Things have got broken between me and Mam and I don't know what can fix it.'

'Find out,' said Stephen promptly.

'Find out what?'

'About your real mother. Someone must know. Mr Dawson, or Auntie May, or even Mrs Liverstitch. Get them to tell you. Then you'll understand how it was for Mam, why she took you in. You'll understand yourself better too. You'll know who you are, and where you belong.'

All the time Stephen was talking, Enoch found himself getting angrier and angrier.

'It's easy for you to say!' he burst out. 'But nobody will tell me anything. And what difference do you think it would make if I did know? My mother is someone worse than Mam. She left me with Mam, didn't she? She didn't want me to know her, so why should I care who she is?'

Suddenly Stephen's arms were round him.

'It's all right,' Stephen murmured. 'It's all right. I didn't mean to upset you. Calm down, Enoch. There's no good talking any more about it tonight.'

As Enoch climbed into bed beside his brother, he wondered how Stephen could be so gentle.

'You should be the minister, not me,' he said quietly.

There was a silence before Stephen answered.

'I have thought about it. What I'd have done if it had been me the money was left to.'

Enoch pushed himself up on his elbow.

'You wouldn't have wanted it, though, would you, Stephen? I mean, you've never been any good at studying.'

'No,' agreed Stephen. 'No, but it might have been a different thing for me. It might have paid my premium to learn a trade.'

Enoch stretched out so that his foot touched his brother's.

'I'm sorry.'

'Not your fault. Grandad hardly knew me. Anyway, who ever said life was fair?'

Enoch shut his eyes tight. When he was earning a

proper wage, he would make life fair to Stephen. That was a promise.

Enoch woke early the next day. It couldn't have been more than five o'clock. The noise of the birds and the early summer light made him feel alert and alive. He left Stephen to sleep while he went downstairs in his socks to get the fire going. As he went into the kitchen Enoch felt there was something different about the room. It was only as he fetched the cups that he noticed what it was. There was a postcard on the mat by the front door. He stared at it. They never got letters. They never sent them. Enoch couldn't remember having ever seen the postman in this part of town. He went over and picked it up. It had a drawing on the front of a posy of flowers. It was addressed to him, and the postmark read Birmingham. Opposite the address were a few words written in a clear round hand. 'Working northwards. See you soon. Lots of love, Polly.'

Enoch traced over the signature with his finger. Polly. After so long, he hardly dared believe it. He did not know what to feel. It was like someone returning from the dead. He heard footsteps on the stairs, and quickly hid the card in his pocket.

'Have you made the tea yet?' said Mam, coming into the room.

'It's just coming,' said Enoch gruffly.

He began to spoon the leaves into the pot. But his hand shook them all over the table.

'What's the matter with you this morning?' his mother demanded. 'We haven't got tea to throw about.'

Enoch ignored her. He shut his eyes a moment, trying to drag out all his frail memories of Polly. There was so little he could remember. And yet she mattered so much to him, more than a sister really ... He opened his eyes suddenly. His mouth formed a silent O of astonishment. And yet, after all, wasn't it obvious? Did everyone know it but him?

'I need to see Stephen a minute,' he said, moving to the stairs.

'Stephen's asleep. Let him alone, can't you?'

But Enoch was already halfway to the bedroom.

He went in, and looked across at the bed. Stephen was lying sprawled in a tangle of covers, his hand flung out over the side.

'Stephen,' said Enoch gently.

'Mmm?'

'Stephen, I think I know who my mother is.'

Stephen sat up suddenly, pushing the hair out of his eyes.

'You do? Who?'

Enoch shook his head.

'I don't want to say until I'm certain. Until I've seen her.'

'Enoch, wait –'

But Enoch wouldn't wait. He didn't even wait to pour the tea. He ran to work before anyone could speak to him.

The postcard was still in Enoch's pocket as he walked over to the Dawsons' in the afternoon. To his delight, it was not the maid but Mrs Dawson who opened the door, her little boy, John, clinging to her skirt.

'Mr Dawson said he might be a little late. Come and sit with us in the garden. Louisa has been making you a daisy chain.'

Enoch smiled and followed her down the hall and out through the side door into the garden. Louisa Dawson was rolling on the grass, kicking her fat four-year-old legs up in the air. The half-finished daisy chain was abandoned on the rug beside her. As soon as she saw Enoch she threw herself at him for a hug. Enoch lifted her high into the air, laughing at her excitement. They smelt so good, the Dawson children. They smelt clean and well-fed and happy. As Enoch put Louisa down, John Dawson staggered up. Enoch gave him a big growly bear hug that extended to

Louisa, and ended with the three of them landing on the grass in a shrieking heap.

'Have a gentle romp, now,' Mrs Dawson said. 'Mind you don't tear your frock, Louisa!'

Enoch got up, and held out his hands to pull the children to their feet.

'You heard your mamma, now. Up we come.'

Louisa went into a sulk at once.

'I'm not taking hold of your hands,' she told Enoch, getting up by herself. 'I don't like them. They're all hard and ugly.'

'Louisa!'

Enoch looked at his hands. They were like any working lad's, callused and stained with clay, the nails worn down to the quick.

'You mustn't call Enoch's hands ugly. Enoch has to work hard for his living.'

'So does Papa, and his hands aren't like that,' Louisa objected.

Mrs Dawson looked so exasperated that Enoch quickly intervened.

'Never mind. She's only cross because we finished the game. Aren't you going to show me your daisy chain, Lou?'

Louisa gave a shriek. 'It isn't finished!'

She snatched it up and ran across the garden. 'Don't

look. You're not to look till I say you can.'

Mrs Dawson sighed. 'My brothers and I were spanked if we spoke like that.'

'She's only four,' Enoch said. 'Let her be. She'll get enough knocks later on.'

'Hallo, hallo!'

The cheerful voice of Mr Dawson came to them across the grass.

Enoch got to his feet, his heart thumping. He hoped he would have the courage to ask the question that was burning inside him.

'It's a pity we have to retreat into the study on such a lovely afternoon,' Mr Dawson said as they went inside. 'Never mind, Enoch, what shall we tackle first? Tacitus, or that new book I gave you to look at, the Cudsworth?'

'Can I show you this?' Enoch interrupted.

He pulled out the postcard.

Mr Dawson took it, frowning. He read it, checked the postmark, and looked at Enoch with a worried face.

'This is the first time I've heard from Polly since she left.' Enoch said eagerly. 'Mr Dawson, I have to ask you –'

'Does Mrs Kirk know about this card?'

Enoch shook his head.

'I really cannot answer any questions you may have about Polly, Enoch. Not without the consent of your mother.'

'She's not my mother!' Enoch said fiercely. 'You know she isn't. Mr Dawson, is Polly my mother, my real mother?'

Mr Dawson stood perfectly still. Only his eyes blinked rapidly, like a cornered animal.

'I said I will answer no questions about Polly!' he said angrily. Then he sighed, and tried to smile.

'Enoch,' he said gently, 'come and sit down.'

Reluctantly, Enoch obeyed.

'You know how fond we have become of you, Mrs Dawson and I.'

Enoch nodded, staring intently down at the dark brown shiny surface of the desk. He thought he could guess what was coming, and it made him afraid.

'We think of you almost as our own. Your family – well, you haven't had the happiest of times with them. Have you considered that as your career progresses you may want to put a little distance between yourself and your beginning here?'

'You mean because I'm illegitimate?'

Enoch's fear made him outspoken, and Mr Dawson looked angry again. But he went on talking calmly.

'If you must be so indelicate. Let me put it very

simply. Really we should have broached this topic before now, but it is so very difficult a subject. Your education as a minister of the Church will help you to rise in society. The time will come when not only your birth mother, but all your family may be an embarrassment to you. Are you really sure you want to keep in touch with Polly?'

Enoch looked at him in shock, almost in disgust. But he realised Mr Dawson was suffering too. Polly had come between them. He turned his head to look out of the study window. He could see Mrs Dawson playing with the two children on the grass. So often recently he wished he had been born a Dawson. Now all that seemed a childish daydream. Had it been Mr Dawson's daydream too?

Slowly, as much to himself as to Mr Dawson, he said:

'If Polly wants to give me up, that's up to her. But if she is my mother, Mr Dawson, I'm not giving her up. And if I rise in life, I shall carry them all up with me, Polly and Stephen.' He hesitated, and added with angry reluctance. 'Yes, even Mam.'

19

Uncle Stephen fights back

Enoch was always the first one home in the evening. Mam expected him to tidy up, and get the meal started. It was a time he usually enjoyed, having the house to himself. Today, however, he could hardly wait for Mam to come home. There wasn't a great deal he needed to do. Stephen had caught a rabbit on the common earlier in the week, and Mam had stewed it with a lot of vegetables. There was still enough left in the pot for tonight. Enoch wiped down the table and swept the floor. He filled the oil lamp and put in a new wick. Then he looked at the basket of mending by Mam's chair. Mam had taught him to sew buttons and to darn, but he felt too fidgety to fiddle with a needle and thread. He went upstairs to his room and looked at the books on his desk. Then he went to the back door and stood looking down the alley. At last Mam came, walking slowly like an old woman, her face grey with exhaustion.

Inside the house, she flopped into a chair, too tired even to take off her hat.

'I thought I was going to faint this afternoon,' she said. 'It gets so hot in that room. We couldn't stop for a minute because they've got this big order on.'

She shut her eyes. Her hair was all grey now, and the bones of her face and her hands looked frail as a bird's.

'Tea?' Enoch offered.

She nodded.

'And put that stew on to heat up. Stephen's not usually late home when there's something worth eating in the house.'

All the time he was making the tea, she just sat, eyes closed, in the chair. Enoch nudged her as he brought her cup.

'Were you asleep?' he asked.

'Nearly.'

'You're not ill, are you, Mam?' Enoch said.

'As if you'd worry,' she said tartly.

'Maybe you're right,' said Enoch, determined not to lose his temper. 'I was only making conversation.'

'Well, I'm fine,' Mam went on. 'Nothing a cup of tea won't mend.'

They drank their tea in silence, Enoch almost bursting with impatience. As soon as Mam put down her cup, Enoch took out Polly's postcard.

'I thought I'd better show you this,' he said. 'Don't start shouting, please, Mam.'

But Mam didn't shout. She looked at the card, turning it over and over.

'I can't read it,' she said. 'Only the name. Does she say she's coming back?'

Enoch nodded.

'Not when, though,' he added.

Mam's face looked anxious and unhappy. She wasn't angry, as Enoch had expected.

'I wish she'd just leave you alone,' she said. 'I thought she had gone, and good riddance. Why does she have to come back and stir everything up? I told her you were better off without her, and haven't I been proved right? You've got a good future ahead of you, Enoch. Between me and Mr Dawson, you're on the right track.'

Enoch was astonished to hear her say it.

'So you think that now, do you? Shame you couldn't give me the benefit of the doubt earlier on.'

'I might not have treated you as gently as may be,

Enoch. But you were a difficult lad, and I had my duty to do. The Bible says we have to do it.'

'I was never difficult! You were the one that was difficult. I could never do anything that pleased you, Mam.'

She looked stricken by that. For a moment it seemed as if she wanted to cry. Then the mask came over her face again and she said harshly:

'The past's the past. There's no point in raking it all over. You're older now. You're on your way. Don't mess up your chances by letting that girl near you.'

But Enoch could not lock away his feelings the way she could. His need was too powerful, too insistent.

'Mam, will you tell me why you talk about Polly like that? Is it true what I'm thinking? Is Polly my mother?'

Before Mam had a chance to speak, Stephen burst in. He was red-faced and out of breath. He went straight up to his brother.

'Enoch,' he said, 'I just saw Harold. He says his dad has gone to law about your money from Grandad. They want it for themselves. They say our grandfather wasn't in his right mind when he left it to you. He promised it to them for the farm, and they're going to have it.'

'The lying hound!' Mam exploded. 'Him and his spendthrift ways. He has no more idea of how to run a farm than he has of running a circus. The only sensible thing your grandfather did in his whole life was to leave his money away from your Uncle Stephen. God knows he had enough of it when the old man was alive.'

'Well, that's their argument,' said Stephen sitting down, and pouring himself some tea. 'They need it, as well, according to Harold. The farm's done really badly this last couple of years.'

'And whose fault is that?' retorted Mam. 'I don't care how bad it is on the land these days. That man never made a profit when times were easy.'

She got to her feet, and pulled her shawl round her.

'You two eat. I'll try and catch Mr Dawson, and see what he can advise. I'm going to fight that uncle of yours tooth and nail. That money belongs to Enoch. I'll burn that farm of his down sooner than let him use our money to build it up.'

She went out, banging the back door.

Enoch and Stephen exchanged glances, and Stephen grinned.

'She's a very Old Testament woman, isn't she?' he said. 'I could just imagine her banging a tent peg into someone's head.'

'I don't know what she thinks Mr Dawson can do,' Enoch said. 'Last I looked, he'd run out of tent pegs.'

But the joke didn't take the edge off his fear, and he shivered.

'You don't think they really can take the money away from me, do you?'

Stephen looked at him unhappily.

'Harold seemed to think it was a certainty. He was horrible about it. All mean and gloating. I nearly punched his fat face in. But let's see what Mr Dawson says. And you see what I mean about Mam, don't you? She's on your side and fighting mad. Now you've got yourself in the newspaper and she's heard you preaching at church, she's started to believe you really could be a vicar. Six months ago, she'd have told you it was all for the best, and sent you off to Isaac Clamp to put your hours up to full time.'

Enoch shook his head.

'I think she was just glad of the excuse to get away. I'd just asked her who my real mother was.'

Stephen was astonished.

'You mean you actually dared – but what did she say?'

'Nothing. You came bursting in, and that was that. Oh, Stephen, what am I going to do? I'm not meant to hammer clay for the rest of my life. Grandad meant me to do better. And I don't think he meant it just for me. It was for all our family.'

Stephen went over to the stove, and began ladling stew onto two plates.

'Let's eat,' he said practically. 'We'll see what Mam has to say when she comes back.'

'I can't eat,' Enoch said, pushing his plate away.

''Course you can,' said Stephen. 'I didn't catch that rabbit to see it wasted. I don't know what those fancy lawyers can do to your money. But if you don't get that stew inside you, you'll have me to deal with, Enoch Kirk. That's a certainty.'

And under his brother's warmly protective gaze, Enoch began to eat, a little comforted.

Mam came back half an hour later.

'Mr Dawson told me we might have to get ourselves a solicitor,' she said. 'God knows how we'll pay the fees. But it'll be over before it's started. Your uncle hasn't got a leg to stand on, Mr Dawson says. So don't worry, Enoch. The law's on our side. They'll back down after they've wasted their cash buying some lawyer a nice new black suit.'

Stephen clapped Enoch on the back.

'There you are, you can stop worrying. Thank God for it. I'm off out, then.'

Enoch was left alone with Mam. After all his fears, he felt weak with gratitude.

'Storm in a teacup,' she said, taking off her hat.

'We'll lose money by it, of course, but your uncle will lose more, and serve him right. Taking family business to lawyers. It's a disgrace.'

'Thanks, Mam,' said Enoch hesitantly.

She turned in surprise. 'Thanks? What for?'

'For being on my side.'

She sat down beside him. He could see from her face that she was struggling with her feelings. At last she spoke.

'When you came to live with me, Enoch, I swore to bring you up as my own. As far as I am concerned you don't have another mother, so you needn't keep asking me. I'm not saying another word about it. But it stuck in my head, what you said about – me never being pleased with you. I was so hard-pressed when you were little. And I was so fearful of you going wrong. But I needn't have worried, need I? You've turned out like my Daniel. He could have been a teacher, if he'd had the chance you've been given. If he'd not had to go down the pit, I'd still have him here.'

Enoch saw the tears shining in her eyes.

'So I'll fight for you to keep that money,' she said fiercely. 'Not just for you, but for Daniel that loved you.' She wiped a hand over her face, and her voice returned with its normal edge.

205

'Now for pity's sake, go and heat me up some of that stew. I'm nearly dead with hunger.'

'Yes, Mam,' said Enoch gently. When he brought her the plate, he let his hand fall on hers for a moment. It was the slightest of signs, but they were both glad of it.

20

Mr Dawson
makes a proposal

Enoch was eating his breakfast in the sunshine on the
step outside the saggar house. A book lay open on his
lap. He was staring down at it, taking in nothing, lost
in thought about what had happened at the Dawsons'
yesterday. Suddenly a shadow fell over the pages of
the book. He looked up and saw Matthew standing in
front of him. Matthew was working as a fireman in
the furnaces of the pottery now. He had put on a lot of
muscle, shovelling coal, and looked more like a man
than a boy. His good-natured face was the same,
though, and Enoch smiled up at him, pleased to see
him.

'Have you heard any more about your money,
Enoch? Stephen said there was a letter this morning,

asking your Mam to go into Burton about it this afternoon.'

'Stephen seems to have told the whole of Gresley,' Enoch said irritably. 'I've already had to talk it over with Isaac and half the saggar makers.'

'You don't mind me asking, do you?' Matthew looked hurt.

Enoch pulled himself together with an effort.

'No, 'course not. They sent for Mam last week too, but that was only something about their bill. Maybe this time they really will tell her what's been decided. I'm trying not to think about it. Mr Dawson says it'll be all right.'

'Oh, good. He'd know, wouldn't he?' Matthew looked relieved. 'Is that one of your books you've got there?' He squinted upside down at the tiny print. 'Looks like poetry.'

Enoch's smile returned. 'It's called *The Iliad*. I wish I could read it in the original Greek, but I'm only doing New Testament Greek with Mr Dawson.'

'Well, I don't suppose you can do everything,' said Matthew. He took another fascinated squint at the book, and then returned to Enoch.

'What I really wanted to tell you was that if the worst comes to the worst, there's a job going where I am. One of the firemen is leaving. I could put in a word for you, and show you the ropes when you start. The money's not bad, and the other lads are all right –'

Enoch stood up and squeezed Matthew's arm.

'You always look out for me, don't you? Thanks, Matthew. Isaac said there wasn't much chance of me going full time under him. Too many full-time lads in the saggar house already. So mention me to your foreman, eh? Tell him what big muscles I have!'

Matthew grinned.

'I already told him. 'Course, he'll get a shock when he sees how puny you really are –'

Enoch grabbed him in a bear hug and they wrestled with the mock-ferocity of young cubs until they fell against one of the big barrels in the yard.

Matthew got to his feet, brushing himself off, and laughing. 'I'd better get back to work. See you tonight, maybe? I'm calling round for Stephen.'

Enoch nodded. 'It'd be good come out with you. I can't seem to concentrate much on studying with all this hanging over me. Thanks, Matthew.'

Enoch turned and climbed the step into the saggar house. The dirt and the noise and the dark were welcome now, a refuge from the confusion of his thoughts. He picked up his sledgehammer and nodded to Isaac. He was ready. He drove the hammer down on the clay with all his might. While he worked he couldn't think. The hammer drove out the worry that he hadn't heard from Polly. It drove out his fear of the lawyers in Burton. It drove out his unease with Mr Dawson. Mr Dawson was his biggest trouble at present. He hadn't even told Stephen what Mr Dawson had said yesterday.

The shift finished all too quickly. Enoch walked home to an empty house. Stephen was still at work, and his mother had left to walk into Burton shortly after breakfast. Her workday shoes and shawl were by her chair in front of the range. The hairbrush and pins were scattered on the table, where she had taken off her hat and re-done her hair just before she left. Enoch knew he should be washing and changing, getting ready to go to Mr Dawson's. It could, after all, be his last lesson. But Enoch was reluctant to face Mr Dawson after the offer he had made.

They had been studying Tacitus again. Suddenly, Mr Dawson broke off his translation of the Latin text.

'Of course,' he said, 'if you do lose your legacy, Enoch, it needn't necessarily mean an end to all this.'

Enoch frowned. 'I can't pay for lessons out of my earnings. The money's needed at home, Mr Dawson.'

He smiled. 'I wasn't thinking of being paid. I was thinking along quite different lines. Mrs Dawson and

I have grown fond of you, Enoch. We don't want to be parted from you now, over a question of mere money. If the worst comes to the worst – or perhaps I should say, if the best comes to the best – and you lose that legacy, we would be happy to take over the responsibility for your education.'

Mr Dawson's face was shining with happiness. Enoch couldn't take it in. He looked away, down at the man's long fingers smoothing the pages of the book.

'I don't understand,' he said. 'You mean, you'd teach me, and send me to the county college and all?'

'Better than that, if we can find the means,' said Mr Dawson. 'There are scholarships for clergy children, Enoch, scholarships to good schools, even to the universities –'

'But I'm not a clergy child,' Enoch said, turning to stare at him.

'You could be.' Mr Dawson had broken into a faint sweat. His smile seemed as if it would burst. 'You could join our family, Enoch. We could adopt you.'

Enoch was stunned. He knew Mr Dawson meant him to be happy. Mr Dawson wanted him to reflect the glow that lit up his own face.

'Of course,' Mr Dawson went on, 'it would mean seeing less of your own family. I have no objection to your brother coming regularly, and you could perhaps visit your old home once a month. But as to pursuing any more distant connections –'

'I would have to give up Polly,' Enoch said. He felt numb. 'Why, Mr Dawson?'

Mr Dawson looked shamefaced. 'We needn't discuss it any further. Actually, I still believe your legacy to be safe. But I wanted to tell you of my plan, to put any worry out of your mind.'

'Thank you, Mr Dawson,' said Enoch softly.

Mr Dawson resumed his translating, and Enoch followed mechanically. He answered Mr Dawson's questions, and began translating in his turn. But he could not meet his tutor's eyes, and when Mr Dawson's sleeve brushed his hand, he drew it away with something like horror.

It was time to go to his lesson, but Enoch sat on at the table, unable to move. He picked up one of his mother's hairpins, and twisted it this way and that. Did Mr Dawson know that Polly was his mother? Enoch was almost certain that he did. Yet he had asked him to give her up.

'He means it for a kindness,' Enoch whispered. 'More than that. He wants me for a son. He'd be giving me all I ever wanted.'

Could he say yes to Mr Dawson? Three weeks ago, it might have been possible. But the postcard had come. He could not ignore it.

'But Polly left me without a word,' he argued to himself. 'I haven't seen her since Daniel's funeral. For all I know Mr Dawson could be right. Mam could be right. What's one stupid postcard worth after all this time?'

But his heart told him otherwise. He could never forget the girl who waited for him at the corner of the street. Polly had loved him then.

'Oh, why isn't she here yet?' he exclaimed aloud. 'If I could just see her, I'd know.'

The hairpin he was twisting broke suddenly and fell in pieces to the floor.

Enoch got up. He had decided what to do. He cut himself some bread, and put it in his pocket. He filled his bottle with cold tea from the pot, and left the house, still in his work clothes. When he reached the church, instead of stopping at the vicarage gate he walked on swiftly, his head down. Mr Dawson would be anxious, but Enoch couldn't help that. He didn't think he could bear to be with Mr Dawson today, and besides, he had a plan to carry out. He kept walking until the pavement gave way to dusty road, and the houses were behind him.

The sun was warm, and he took off his coat and carried it over his shoulder. He picked up a stick, and swung it as he walked, slashing at the nettles and strong grass shooting up at the roadside. Mam would know by now. Her appointment was for eleven o'clock. She might come for him at the Dawsons', and then there would be a row. But he couldn't worry about that. Before he found out about the money, before he decided anything about the future, he had to find out if Polly really was his mother. He was going to ask someone who would surely tell him the truth.

Enoch began to run. His boots sent the dust up off the road behind him, as he ran past the red clay pits and the heather of the common. He took the same road he had taken with Mr Dawson years ago. When he reached the turning for the farm, he stopped to rest. He drank thirstily from the bottle of tea, but he couldn't eat. He went on again, slowly now. The ground sloped suddenly, and the farm came into view. The familiar jumble of buildings shocked him. He stood still for a moment, taking it in. He had lived here. Now he stood outside it. It was like the childish handwriting in his old schoolbooks, his and not his.

He began to walk down the track towards the farmhouse. As he got closer, he saw that it was shabbier than he remembered. The whitewash on the walls was dingy and peeling. The window boxes on either side of the front door were empty. The yard was scattered with bits of rusting machinery around which the hens were pecking. Enoch began to feel nervous. He reached the gate and a dog began to bark. It came bounding up towards him across the muddy yard, a great black brute of a thing, showing its teeth. At once the door of the farmhouse opened.

'If it's more of you with your letters and threats, you're out of luck,' a shrill woman's voice shouted. 'He's not here, and Mr Harold's not here, so you'll have to take your business elsewhere.'

'Auntie?' said Enoch, shocked and uncertain.

The troubles of the last couple of years had changed her terribly. She was the same comfortable shape as he remembered, but her hair was grey now, and flopped untidily round her face. She was wearing a shabby brown dress, and her apron was old and torn. She walked slowly down the yard towards him, and as she grew nearer he saw fear in her face.

'I've got this dog, now, so don't you think of arguing with me,' she said with a ferocity her eyes denied.

'Auntie,' said Enoch in distress. 'It's me. It's Enoch.'

'Enoch?'

She didn't smile. If anything, the worry lines on her face deepened.

'How are you, Auntie May? How's the family? Aren't you going to open the gate and let me in?'

She was still holding on to the dog's collar.

'Your uncle isn't home,' she repeated.

Enoch felt himself going red. 'That doesn't matter. I didn't come to see him. I came to see you.'

'Well, I can't tell you anything. It was all your uncle's idea, and Harold backed him up. I don't want to take your money, but your uncle says it's our only chance of keeping the farm.'

Enoch's blush deepened. 'It's not about the money. Honestly, Auntie May.'

Still she seemed to hesitate, then at last swung open the gate.

'Friend, Jack, friend, all right?' she said to the dog. The dog looked at Enoch in disgust and turned away.

As they walked towards the house, Auntie May pushed back her hair and glanced down at her apron.

'We're a bit at sixes and sevens these days,' she said. 'Nell went home to her mother for a bit of a holiday. We decided it was better to try to keep the men on. It's not as if I can't manage on my own in the house. Only if I'm doing the rough work, there's not much point dressing smartly.'

She turned to him as they reached the front door. 'Harold's still in that same bedroom he used to share with you. Only Edy's not with us now, of course.'

'She got married, didn't she? Stephen told me.'

Auntie May nodded.

'It's nice to see her properly settled. Thomas Cowan, her husband, has got a really good position in the office at Allsopp's Brewery. Of course, we don't see so much of them, these days.'

'No, I suppose not,' said Enoch lamely. He felt so sad at the change in Auntie May he could hardly keep up this exchange of family news.

To his relief, the inside of the house looked just as he remembered it.

'You've still got those shepherds and shepherdesses, then,' he said, looking over at the china on the mantelpiece.

She nodded distractedly. Her hands twisted her apron a little.

'I'll make us some tea in a minute, if you like, and we can get comfortable.'

She cleared her throat, and looked slightly away from him. 'First off, though, Enoch, the thing you have to remember is that Stephen expected that money to go to Harold. The old man always spoke in front of us as if that's what he intended. You can't blame Stephen, not with the way things are for farmers at present.'

Enoch nodded uncomfortably. 'Really, Auntie May,

I don't want to talk about it. I know it's not your fault.'

She looked at him, her face clearing. 'So what have you come for, Enoch?'

He twisted his hands round his cap. Now that the moment had come, he was scared. He looked past her, out of the window, where the sun showed up the failure of the farm.

'I want to know who my mother is,' he said. 'I want to know if it's Polly.'

Auntie May sat down rather suddenly at the table.

'How did you find out? Not from Ellen, surely.'

'She didn't mean to tell me,' he said. 'Auntie May, you've always been kind. Can't you understand how much I need to know?'

She stared at him, her tired soft face looking troubled.

'I don't want to be the one to tell you,' she said. 'Not if your – if Ellen hasn't seen fit to say.'

'I need to know.'

Enoch was no longer afraid. He would stand in front of her, immovable as a rock, until she told him.

Auntie May sighed.

'Well, I don't see what help it'll be to you. It's years ago that she left. Polly is your mother, Enoch. She got into trouble with a soldier, and he went away and left her.'

'Polly is my mother.'

It felt strange to his mouth to say it. He was happy and angry at the same time.

'She left me,' he blurted out like a little child. 'She left me, and she didn't say goodbye.'

He began to cry, hard painful sobs like retches. He bent over, drowning in the force of his grief. He felt Auntie May's arm come down on his shoulder and shook it off violently.

'Leave me alone. Leave me alone!'

'Enoch, Enoch, I'm trying to tell you,' Auntie May was saying. 'Enoch, she didn't.'

At last he heard her.

'Didn't what?' he said fiercely.

'Didn't go without saying goodbye. She came here, to the farm. I wouldn't let her in to see you. So she left a letter.'

He looked at her with such anger that she flinched.

'It – it said how much she loved you, and that she was going to come back for you when she could. She made me promise to tell you, but of course I didn't. It was for the best, Enoch. Your life is here, with respectable folk. God knows where Polly is now.'

'Where's the letter?' he demanded. 'I want to see it.'

Auntie May shook her head.

'It's gone, Enoch. I didn't think to keep it.'

'But she promised to come back for me. She sent her love.'

He felt an intense joy. She hadn't forgotten him, any more than he had forgotten her. Each had lived in the other's heart, more than a memory, a living passion.

'And after all, what was the point in upsetting you, when I knew she would never come back?' Auntie May was saying. 'Running off with that man. I don't suppose it lasted six weeks. There were other letters that came in the post, once or maybe twice a year. Your uncle put them straight on the fire. There's been nothing this year though. She's dead, most likely, Enoch. And she was such a bright little thing! But everything went wrong for her. I thought you were going to stay with us, remember, Enoch. I thought of you almost as my own. I didn't want you all upset by false promises.'

Enoch smiled. His rage was swallowed up in joy and relief.

'But it wasn't a false promise,' he said. 'I've heard from her, Auntie May. Polly'll be here soon.'

Auntie May gasped, and her hand went to her throat.

'Don't tell Ellen I told you anything, for pity's sake.

She's got enough against us as it is. Please, Enoch. Don't tell her.'

Enoch nodded. All he wanted now was to be alone with what he knew.

'I'd better go,' he said abruptly. 'Mam thinks I'm at Mr Dawson's, and as it is I'll be late home.'

Auntie May followed him out of the house and down as far as the gate. She seemed reluctant to part with him.

'Well – bye, then,' Enoch said, as he opened the gate to go.

'You're not still cross with me, are you?' Auntie May said anxiously.

Enoch kissed her soft cheek.

'It was stupid of me to be angry,' he said. 'You told me what I need to know.'

She kissed him back, and then took him in his arms for a proper hug. 'It was lovely to see you,' she said. 'You know I'm always here in the day when the men are out. Always here.'

She stood watching while he walked off up the track. He stopped to wave once, and she waved back, looking lost and lonely in her own front yard. He didn't expect to come back. They both knew it.

21

What happened in Burton

When Enoch reached home, he looked in at the window. Mam was already there. He stood outside, bracing himself to go in and face her. He would have to talk about the money before he could talk about Polly. But he only needed to look at her to see how the trip into Burton had ended. Mam was sitting all bunched up in her chair, still in her Sunday clothes, only minus her coat and hat. She was staring straight ahead. She didn't get up as he came into the house. She didn't even turn round. She waited for him to come right up to her before she spoke.

'Well, aren't you going to ask me?'

'I don't need to ask,' Enoch said quietly. 'The money's gone, isn't it?'

She nodded, and her mouth trembled. The tears began to escape out of her eyes, faster than she could wipe them away.

'What have we done?' she said. 'What have we done, that every little bit of hope is taken away from us? Why is God testing us like this? First Robert, then Daniel, and now this for you. It isn't fair, Enoch. It isn't fair.'

She was crying like a little girl. It seemed suddenly simple to kneel down and put his arm round her.

'It's all right, Mam,' he said. 'It's all right. I'll manage. It's not the end of the world.'

She let herself be held.

'That man,' she said, 'That solicitor. He was polite enough. But it meant nothing to him, whether we won or lost. I wanted to break up his office, and shout at him, "Now have I made you care?"'

'Like Samson,' said Enoch. He couldn't help smiling at the thought of it.

She pulled herself upright, scrubbing at her eyes.

'I don't know what there is to laugh at,' she said resentfully. 'You just tell me what you're going to do now. And Mr Dawson will have to be told.'

Enoch stood up to face her.

'Mr Dawson's offered to take me in,' he told her. 'More than that, to adopt me.'

As she stared at him in shock, he added quickly:

'I'm going to turn him down, though.'

She was silent for a moment.

'But you've no other chance of getting on, Enoch. He offered you that, and you've said no? Why, for pity's sake? You practically live there as it is. If they take you in, they'll treat you as their own. It's not just a chance to go on studying. You'll learn their way of talking, their manners. You'll have their class behind you. That'll really help you to get on. It's a better chance than you had before.'

Enoch studied her earnest face. This time she really did seem to want only what was best for him. It was hard for him to believe it. 'You'd be happy to see me go?'

'No, not happy, exactly. But what have I got to offer you instead? I know which I'd choose if I were you.'

Slowly Enoch shook his head. 'He wanted me to give up my family, and I can't do that.'

'I'd have thought you couldn't put us lot behind you quick enough,' she said with an awkward laugh. 'We've never been much use to you.'

'That's not true, Mam,' said Enoch gently. He hesitated, before taking her hand. 'There's a lot I'd wish had been different. There's a lot of times I can't think about without it hurting. But you can't unpick your life like a bit of knitting. It's God who can sort that out, not us. I'm part of this family, and I'm not ashamed of who I am. Mr Dawson thinks I should be. He's in the wrong.'

'But what about your books?' she lamented. 'What about your future?'

Enoch sighed.

'There's other places to study,' he said, trying to sound braver than he felt. 'There's the public library in Burton, when I can get over there. There's the Mechanics Institute. Maybe Mr Dawson will go on helping me a little. It would be very unchristian of him to bear a grudge, after all. If I go on trying, somebody will notice me, and lend me a hand. I'll get my training, Mam. I'm still going to be a minister and go out into the world.'

Mam looked at him in silence, her hand still closed tightly on his own.

'I was wrong about you,' she said at last. 'I thought you were weak, and liable to go wrong, just because of how you got made and born. But you're stronger than I am.'

'No. It runs in the family.' He took a deep breath and said it. 'From you down to Polly and on to me.'

She gave a wry smile. 'I was shocked when you

asked me the other day. I should have realised you'd work it out.'

'It could only be Polly,' Enoch said. 'Mr Dawson can't keep me from my own mother. He's wrong to try.'

She looked at him for a long moment in silence. Then she gave a nod.

'Fetch my handbag.'

'What for?' Enoch demanded, irritated at this descent into the mundane.

'Always at your questions! Just do what I ask, can't you?'

He went to find the bag and dumped the black battered thing on her lap with an ill grace. She ignored this, and scrabbled about in the bag, talking as she searched.

'I was going to burn this,' she said. 'I thought it was the best thing to do. I sent her away, and I meant her to stay away from you. But your life seems to have its own shape, not the one I marked out for you. Here it is. You'd better see what it says.'

She held out a coloured postcard. Enoch took it in shaking hands.

'She's in Burton,' he said. 'She's in some show at the Theatre Royal. She'll be there tonight. Where's the Theatre Royal, Mam? Tell me, for pity's sake.'

'You're not going to try and get there now?' Mam looked appalled. 'She'll make her way her in a day or two, I'm sure.'

'It doesn't say that on the card.' Enoch made an agitated movement with his arms. 'Mam, I can't just sit and wait.'

Her expression was unreadable.

'You'd better go, then.'

Enoch grabbed his cap.

'What about eating?' she asked him.

He felt in his pocket.

'I've got that sixpence Stephen owed me. I'll buy something there.'

'Enoch.' Mam got up and went over to him. 'Enoch, before you go. I need to tell you how it was. Otherwise, when you and Polly talk – I just don't want you to think badly of me, that's all.'

He could barely stand still, but he forced himself to sit down at the table near her. His fingers fidgeted with the breadcrumbs as she began.

'Polly got leave to come and see us just after the accident. Her dad was killed, and I thought Daniel was dying. The miners told me we'd be getting compensation money. But the bosses made out we were owed nothing. I never understood it. I don't remember that time very well. I think I was very nearly mad with it all. I didn't know how we were going to live. Then Polly told me she was expecting. She'd kept it well hidden, and she had her job to go back to. Just as well. I wouldn't and I couldn't take her in. She never told me about the father. The baby came – you came – while she was staying with us. So I kept you. It was that or the workhouse, Enoch. Polly couldn't keep you and feed herself.'

Enoch pushed the breadcrumbs away with angry fingers. He wanted to cry, but his eyes were hot and dry.

'Maybe I was wrong to stop her seeing you. But I wanted to raise you right. I felt so ashamed of her, Enoch!'

He felt her hard hands come down gently on his shoulders.

'But somehow it's all turned out different from what I expected. I'm not sorry you came, Enoch. For a long time I let you pay for the bad things that had happened. If you'd chosen the Dawsons, I couldn't blame you. But you've stuck with us, and with Polly too. And I'm glad of it.'

Then at last the tears came. His mouth shook and he began to cry. And with her hands on his shoulders, Mam cried with him.

22

Polly

It was late when Enoch got to Burton, and later still by the time that he found his way to the Theatre Royal. There were already people coming out, crowds of them. He pushed his way inside, to be stopped by a burly man dressed like a bandmaster in a scarlet coat with immense gold epaulettes.

'Show's over, lad. Or did someone ask you to fetch them a cab?'

'No, no,' Enoch struggled to get his breath and speak. 'I know someone in the show, that's all. I was to meet them –'

'They'd have told you to try the stage door, then, wouldn't they?'

The man seemed to grow bigger, and rather

menacing. His eyes were hostile above his jolly black moustache.

'Small door round the back of the theatre. Mind you have bona fide credentials. Old Jack doesn't let many through.'

Enoch let the crowd carry him back through the door on to the pavement outside. The crush here seemed worse if anything. The front of the theatre was brightly lit, but Enoch could see nothing but people. No one seemed ready to go home. Ladies stood holding their skirts close to them, chattering while their gentlemen whistled for cabs. A barefoot tousled girl went from group to group, hand held out, her voice a whispered whine. Most of them ignored her, but she persisted. She glanced at Enoch, and glanced away. No chance of a penny there. Enoch grabbed her thin shoulder.

'Let go of me!'

'No, listen. Where's the stage door? Show me, and you can have this.'

He held out the pork pie he'd bought to eat himself.

She snatched it from him, took a bite of the shiny brown crust.

'Down there, look.' She pointed with a dirty hand to an alley that ran along the side wall of the theatre. 'At the bottom. You can't mistake it.'

He left her gobbling the pie, and pushed his way through to the entrance of the dark alley.

It was a relief to leave the noise and the light behind. There was a single dim gas jet burning over a door at the bottom of the alley. He walked towards it, stumbling over rubbish as he went. When he got to the door, he saw it was slightly open. His knock made the door swing inwards. A voice like a cracked bell sang out:

'Name and business, please!'

Enoch peered in, trying to see who had spoken.

A tiny old man was sitting on a stool in the doorway. Old Jack had a wispy pointed beard, and his eyes glittered with malice like a malevolent pixie. Enoch's heart sank at the look of him, but he spoke with all the confidence he could muster.

'I want to see Polly Kirk, please,'

'There's no one of that name here,' retorted the old man.

'But she asked me to come and see her!'

'You'd be surprised how many people tell me that,' Old Jack replied with maddening calm. 'I don't even know your name yet. Name and business, I said.'

Enoch took a breath. If he lost his temper he would get nowhere.

'I'm Enoch Kirk and Polly Kirk is who I want to

see.' A terrible thought struck him. 'She might have another name here. A – a stage name, they call it, don't they?'

'They do,' the old man agreed. 'And it's more than likely, for there's no Pollys here. But if I don't know who you want, I can't fetch'em for you, can I?'

'I'll tell you what she looks like,' Enoch said desperately. 'She will want to see me, I promise. She's got fair hair, and blue eyes and she's quite young and pretty –'

'So that rules out the fat old ladies. Only ninety-seven females to go. I don't suppose you know what act she's in?'

Enoch shut his eyes. He tried to remember.

'She was with a magician,' he said finally. 'She could be working in his act.'

The old man nodded, but his watery eyes gave nothing away.

'Enoch Burke, was it?'

'Kirk. Kirk!' Enoch shouted.

The old man slid off his stool.

'I'll see if I can find you an answer,' he said imperturbably.

His slippered feet flapped away down the dim corridor.

Enoch shut his eyes and leaned back against the

cold brick wall of the alley. He was ready to faint with hunger and tiredness. All the way to Burton he had been talking to Polly in his head. He had run at top speed, explaining as he went. He had not stopped to think. When he could no longer run, his lungs bursting and his legs trembling with weakness, he forced himself to walk, to keep moving. He was afraid to stop. When he stopped the doubts would come. And now, waiting in the dark, his fear was overwhelming. Perhaps she would not know him any more. Perhaps they would be like strangers. He might go away without daring to tell her what he knew. Worst of all, if the old man could not find her, if the old man did not let him in, Polly might go without ever knowing he had come.

Suddenly there was noise again behind the door. The old man's cracked voice and flapping feet, but another voice too:

'Enoch! I was going to come tomorrow, but you found me first!'

It was Polly's voice, but it wasn't Polly. He was looking at a stranger, a lovely girl, scented and pretty. Her legs and arms were bare and her clothes were made of glittery scratchy stuff and feathers, and her face was bold with colours. 'Don't be shocked,' she said in Polly's voice. 'Please don't look so shocked. It's only my stage costume. I didn't have time to change. When I heard you were at the door, I just wanted to run –'

She reached out her hand, and Enoch took it. Then everything was all right, because it was Polly's hand. Their eyes met, and Enoch felt a surge of love and pride. She must know that I know, he thought.

'Come inside,' Polly said. 'We can talk in my dressing room.'

Enoch held tightly on to her hand as she led him down the corridor. He tried not to stare as they met a tall man the colour of chocolate, and a tiny woman as small as a four year old. Polly smiled and said something at each of the open doors they passed. Glancing in, Enoch saw men and women, half changed, or still in glittering costumes. He was shocked and enchanted by this world Polly moved at ease in. He wondered uneasily how he could relate to it.

At last they came to Polly's dressing-room. But to Enoch's dismay, there was a man in it, standing at the mirror, wiping his face with a cloth. Polly tugged at his sleeve.

'Alfie, Alfie!' she exclaimed. 'Enoch's here. We shan't have to go looking for him after all.'

The man turned round. Enoch saw he was in

evening dress. He had a foreign look, with his dark skin, crisp black hair and shiny black moustache. He let out a yell, and was across the room in a second. Enoch was amazed to find himself being hugged.

'So she's got you at last!' said Alfie.

He gave Enoch a clap on the back, and turned to Polly.

'I'll be next door with Stefano and Big Mick,' he said, kissing her on the cheek. 'If your boy wants to stay the night at our digs, he's more than welcome.'

Your boy, Enoch thought in wonder. He called me Polly's boy.

He turned to Polly. Now they were alone she too seemed nervous. Somehow it was hard to start talking about what was uppermost in their minds.

'Have a seat,' said Polly. 'Only mind the rabbit cage. Put all those silk scarves in the corner on top of the hamper. Alfie's a great magician, but he's no good at tidying up.'

'Where's he from, your Alfie?' Enoch asked.

'Liverpool,' said Polly. 'But his father was from Barbados.'

'A black man?' said Enoch, feeling very ignorant.

Polly nodded. 'And his mother's family are from Romania, from a gypsy family. They're the ones with the circus connection.'

Enoch's head was beginning to spin. He tried to find some common ground.

'Well, I like him. He seemed very pleased to see me.'

Polly laughed. 'He's had to put up with me talking about you ever since we left Gresley. Oh, Enoch, I'm sorry it took so long for me to come back to you. But while we were in London we had no money, and then the baby came. I sent letters to the farm, but you never wrote back. Then I thought perhaps you went back to live with Mam. That's why I sent the postcards there.'

Enoch took a deep breath.

'The postcards were all I got,' he said.

Polly looked at him, appalled.

'Not – not when I left? You didn't even get that one? They let you think I just disappeared. Oh, Enoch. Oh, my poor lad.'

She came and knelt by his chair and took his hands.

'I would never abandon you,' she said protectively. 'Mam tried to make me. She said you were better off without me. But I knew that couldn't be true.'

Enoch looked at the hands clasping his own.

'I couldn't be better off without my own mother,' he said.

Polly tightened her grip. Her eyes were shining with tears.

Then he was in her arms at last in a hug that outweighed out the world.

23

A new life

'So there she is,' said Polly. 'Your half-sister.'

Enoch looked at the small child curled up asleep in the big bed. She was remarkably pretty, with soft brown curly hair and golden skin.

'Alfie's mother looks after her when we're at the theatre,' Polly said. 'When she's a bit bigger Alfie wants to her to come on stage with us. I've told him, so long as it doesn't affect her schooling. Education's important, specially for girls.'

'I can't believe you called her Ellen,' Enoch said.

Polly smiled.

'Alfie loves that name. And I didn't mind. Mam quarrelled with me, not the other way round. I was bitter enough when I was younger, but not now.

How can I be angry with anyone, when I've got so much?'

They went back into the sitting-room and sat down side by side. Polly's lodgings were in a big shabby house not far from the theatre. Alfie's mother had supper waiting for them, and other members of the show wandered in from their own rooms, bringing bottles and dishes to share. During the noisy supper Enoch told Polly as much as he could about Grandad and the legacy, and how his chance of studying was gone. Now it was past midnight. Polly and Enoch were alone again, but there was still the sound of talk and laughter all over the house.

'You look very tired, Enoch,' Polly said with a look of concern. 'I hope it hasn't all been too much. It's just Alfie wanted everyone to meet you. They're a lovely crowd on this show, but they're very different from Gresley folk.'

Enoch grinned, and rubbed his eyes.

'Well, I've never seen Mr Dawson pick up the teacups and juggle with them. It's amazing, but don't you ever feel like a bit of quiet?'

Polly laughed.

'It'll be quieter when we are back in London. We're going back to our regular act in the music hall. We're high up on the bill – second featured act, Enoch – and we earn enough not to have to struggle any more.'

She reached out and took his hand. 'Enoch, I've been waiting to say this for so long. It's what I've dreamed of for years and years. Will you come back with us to London? I know theatre people are not what you're used to. I know you'll find it strange at first. But we can afford to send you to school. I've talked to Alfie, and what's ours is yours, just as much as it is little Ellen's. There are good schools in London. We can go round them all, and find the best for you. Oh, you'll love London, Enoch. There's museums and libraries, the best in the world. You'll be able to go to St Paul's for a sermon one day, and to college for a lecture by some great scientist the next. You'll have the best chance to learn there is.'

She squeezed his hand tightly.

'But the most important thing is that we'll be together. I don't want to lose you now that I've found you again.'

Enoch was in tears.

'I want to be with you, Polly,' he said softly. 'I will come. The Dawsons will miss me, I think, but they've got their own children. They'll get over it. But what about Stephen and Mam? Do you think they'll be all right if I leave them?'

Polly pulled him closer so that his head was resting on her shoulder.

'London's not so far away,' she said. 'You'll have holidays, you know. I don't want to part you from anyone you love.'

A fire had been lit in the grate for, though it was summer, the evenings were still cold.

They sat watching the flames together.

'I think Mam will be glad you've called your baby Ellen,' Enoch said after a while. 'She's sorry. I think she wishes things had been different.'

Polly looked at him in such wonder that they both laughed.

'I'd love to see her again, if she'll see me. Will you ask her, Enoch?'

'Of course, Mum.'

She pushed the fringe out of his eyes.

'All the bad things,' she said. 'They don't seem to have hurt you. I had to leave you with Mam, you know? I couldn't keep you. And I prayed you'd be all right. Every night I prayed for you, Enoch. It's the only thing in my life I've ever prayed for.'

Enoch kissed her wet cheek, then leaned back against her side.

He watched the fire, thinking of all the days they would have together till he grew up.

'I am very lucky,' he said. 'I have been so loved.'

Afterword

This book is based on real events.

Enoch Kirk was my great-grandfather and as an old man in the 1930s, he wrote down the story of his life. That big black ledger, hand-written in blue ink, passed from his son to his granddaughter, my mother, and then to me. When I read what he had written, I knew wanted to make a story out of it.

Many of the characters and events in *Just a Boy* are unchanged from my great-grandfather's account. Mam and Daniel and the family at the farm were real people. His early childhood was the harsh one in the book, and he did get the chance of an education through some money left by his loving grandfather. Sadly, when his uncle snatched the money back, there was no Polly to rescue to him. The real Enoch joined the army and served in the Royal Army Medical Corps. He achieved his dream of seeing the world, travelling as far as the West Indies, Nigeria and South Africa.

He died just before the Second World War. Somehow I still feel very close to him.

Maeve Henry

2001

LISTEN TO THE DARK

BY MAEVE HENRY

Winner of the Smarties Prize

*'He could not think about what
had happened in the park, only
remember his fear and his flight, the
desperate scramble over the railings.
Now it was here with him, he could feel
it, the thing he had run away from.'*

Mark Robson is a loner. Bullied at
school, suffocated at home, he just
doesn't fit.

But suddenly he finds himself haunted
by a secret from the past.

There is no one he can confide in.

Nothing will be the same again.

A GIFT FOR A GIFT

BY MAEVE HENRY

*'Suddenly all the birds in the room
were alive, beating at the walls of their
glass cases or flying free. Fran covered
her head to protect it from the
frantic wings and dreadful noise.'*

One night, in despair and anger at her
family, Fran storms out of her home
and seeks refuge in what seems to be
an empty house. But there she meets
the strange and elusive Michael, who
has the power to grant her any wish,
but who, in return, insists on a gift of
his own choosing – that Fran will stay
with him in this life and beyond.